Jim felt the babies move.

He splayed his hand on Teresa's stomach, amazed that she could sleep so soundly while the babies wriggled and kicked. Amazed that these movements were made by his children.

He lay next to her on the bed, on top of the covers, his hand still covering her belly. He told himself he just wanted to understand how a husband would feel. How would it feel to hold the future in his hands?

Would Teresa understand if she awoke? Could he convince her he was sharing a moment with the babies?

A moment with the babies? asked that annoying voice inside his head. *Or a moment with the babies' mother?*

Jim scoffed at the suggestion. He was getting married to give his babies a name. That was the only reason.

Wasn't it?

Dear Reader,

To me, September is the cruelest month. One minute it feels like just another glorious summer day. And then almost overnight the days become shorter and life just hits. It's no different for this month's heroes and heroines. Because they all get their own very special "September moment" when they discover a secret that will change their lives forever!

Judy Christenberry once again heads up this month with *The Texan's Tiny Dilemma* (#1782)—the next installment in her LONE STAR BRIDES miniseries. A handsome accountant must suddenly figure out how to factor love into the equation when a one-night stand results in twins. Seth Bryant gets his wake-up call when a very pregnant princess shows up on his doorstep in *Prince Baby* (#1783), which continues Susan Meier's BRYANT BABY BONANZA. Jill Limber assures us that *The Sheriff Wins a Wife* (#1784) in the continuing BLOSSOM COUNTY FAIR continuity, *but* how will this lawman react to the news that he's still married to a woman who left town eight years ago! Holly Jacobs rounds out the month with her next PERRY SQUARE: THE ROYAL INVASION! title. In *Once Upon a King* (#1785), baby seems to come before love and marriage for a future king.

And be sure to watch for more great romances next month when bestselling author Myrna Mackenzie launches our new SHAKESPEARE IN LOVE miniseries.

Happy reading,

Ann Leslie Tuttle
Associate Senior Editor

Please address questions and book requests to:
Silhouette Reader Service
U.S.: 3010 Walden Ave., P.O. Box 1325, Buffalo, NY 14269
Canadian: P.O. Box 609, Fort Erie, Ont. L2A 5X3

JUDY
Christenberry

The Texan's Tiny
Dilemma

Lone Star
Brides

SILHOUETTE *Romance*®

Published by Silhouette Books

America's Publisher of Contemporary Romance

SILHOUETTE BOOKS

ISBN 0-373-19782-9

THE TEXAN'S TINY DILEMMA

Copyright © 2005 by Judy Russell Christenberry

Visit Silhouette Books at www.eHarlequin.com

Printed in U.S.A.

Books by Judy Christenberry

JUDY CHRISTENBERRY

has been writing romances for over fifteen years because she loves happy endings as much as her readers do. She's a bestselling author for Harlequin American Romance, but she has a long love of traditional romances and is delighted to tell a story that brings those elements to the reader. A former high school French teacher, Judy devotes her time to writing. She hopes readers have as much fun reading her stories as she does writing them. She spends her spare time reading, watching her favorite sports teams and keeping track of her two adult daughters.

Prologue

Teresa Tyler wearily eased away from the toilet. She'd been sick every morning for the past two weeks.

At first, she'd thought she had a touch of the flu. But now she had more than a niggling feeling her first guess had been wrong. Steadying her nervous hands, she withdrew the small box from the drugstore sack and carefully read the directions. They were supposed to be easy, or so the manufacturer said. Right now nothing seemed simple.

After she followed the two-step process, she paced the floor of her house, waiting the allotted time. But she knew what the results would show. To be honest, she'd figured it out pretty quickly, even though it hadn't happened to her before.

Nor had she planned for it to happen. Not at all,

which was stupid on her part. She'd been so wrapped up in the throes of love that her actions had seemed so natural, absolutely perfect.

Time was up. She picked up the test strip and looked at her fate.

She was pregnant.

Chapter One

At four months pregnant, Teresa Tyler didn't move as quickly as she used to. So when the phone rang she needed three rings to answer it.

"I just realized I haven't seen you for more than a month. Why don't you come for dinner this evening?" It was her sister Tommie. She took being the eldest of the triplet sisters seriously and at times acted more like Teresa's mother than her sibling. "I've invited Tabitha and Mom, with Joel, of course, and Pete's mother and brother. It'll be a family night. Say you'll come."

Panic instantly filling her, Teresa replied immediately. "I can't."

"But, Teresa—"

Teresa drew a deep breath. She'd known this day

would come sometime. Tonight was probably as good as any to reveal her secret. "I'll come on one condition."

"What's that?" Tommie asked.

"If you and Tabitha come to lunch today. Just us girls."

Tommie hesitated. Then she said, "Okay. I'll call Tabitha."

"Great. I'll see you both at noon."

After she hung up the phone, Teresa sighed deeply. It was almost a relief that she finally had to tell her sisters the truth. It was inevitable. She couldn't avoid them forever. Besides, she needed Tommie and Tabitha on her side when she faced her mother tonight.

But first things first. How was she going to tell her sisters that she was pregnant and had every intention of raising her baby alone?

On the way, Tommie Tyler Schofield picked up her sister Tabitha. "Have you actually seen Teresa lately?"

"Why, no. She's spending all her spare time working on her book. Which isn't easy after teaching all day."

"So she *is* teaching? One of the women who moved with Pete's company told me Teresa wasn't at the same school anymore."

"What? She never mentioned a change of school to me. Isn't that strange?"

"Pete thinks it's because we keep trying to interfere in her life. He warns me about that all the time," Tommie said with irritation as she parked her car at Teresa's small but well-tended house.

"He just doesn't understand," Tabitha said, getting out of the car. "We've always taken care of Teresa. I know she's only six minutes younger than me but… it's just like you taking charge though you're only two minutes older than me."

"Well, I'm glad we're going to see her today, so we can figure out what's wrong."

They walked up the sidewalk and knocked on the front door.

Teresa swung open the door, wearing jeans and a long work shirt over a white T-shirt. "Come in," Teresa said as she hugged her sisters. She'd missed them the past few weeks.

"How are you?" Tommie asked.

"Fine," Teresa said as she turned to go to the kitchen.

"You look like you've put back on the weight you lost," Tabitha commented. "We were concerned."

Ignoring the remark Teresa waved them toward the breakfast table that was set for three. "Have a seat. I'll explain everything to you."

Taking the homemade quiche from the oven, she cut it into slices and put it on individual plates next to a fresh garden salad. After she'd poured iced tea for all of them, she sat down at the table, only to find both her sisters staring at her.

"I have a lot to confess," Teresa began. "First of all, I'm not teaching."

That revelation took both her sisters by surprise.

"Not at all? We'd discovered you weren't at your old school, but—" Tommie's voice trailed off.

"How are you supporting yourself?" Tabitha asked, getting to the bottom line quickly.

"I'm living on my savings. I took a sabbatical from my job so I could devote myself to my writing."

"So you invited us here to tell us you sold your children's book?" Tommie asked, hoping for the best.

"No, not yet. My other piece of news is…is a little more dramatic. You see, I'm pregnant."

Stunned silence filled the room and echoed in her ears for a full minute.

Finally Tommie asked, "Are you getting married?"

"And to whom?" Tabitha wanted to know.

Teresa stared at the quiche rather than her sisters. "No, I'm not going to marry."

"Why not?" Tommie asked.

"Because the baby and I are a family. We don't need anyone else. Other than you two and Mom, of course."

"But I don't understand," Tommie said. "You loved this man enough to make a baby, but you don't want to marry him?"

"Things didn't work out, Tommie. It happens." She rose from her seat and did some busy work at the counter. Then she turned back to her sister. "Look, I didn't want to come to your house this evening and shock you in front of other people."

"Do you need anything?" Tabitha asked. "What can we do to help?"

"I didn't tell you because I needed your help. I told you because I wanted you to know…and to share in my happiness."

"Oh, we do, sweetie," Tommie said, getting up to hug her sister.

Tabitha did the same.

When they returned to their chairs, Tommie asked in an offhand fashion, "How far along are you?"

"About four months."

"It was that guy you were dating when I got married!" Tommie exclaimed. "I never liked him."

"You didn't date for very long, did you?" Tabitha asked. "I only saw you with him a couple of times."

"No, it—" Teresa caught herself, then, her stomach sinking, she covered up her stammer. "No, it didn't work out." She picked up her fork and dug into her food like a lumberjack on his lunch hour. "Let's eat, before our quiche gets cold."

It was with reluctance that Jim Schofield approached his brother's home that evening. The dinner wasn't just for the Schofields, but also for Tommie's family. Would Teresa be there? He wondered. It'd been months since he'd seen her, and he was filled with mixed feelings at seeing her now.

Before he could gather himself, his mother, whom he'd driven there, reached the front door ahead of him and rang the bell. Evelyn Schofield was so pleased with Pete's marriage and considered herself lucky to have such a thoughtful daughter-in-law. He was grateful for Tommie, too; she now helped out with Evelyn's demands, freeing him from responsibility.

Pete opened the door with an odd look on his face. "Come on in. We were beginning to worry about you. You're the last ones to arrive."

Jim apologized before his mother could complain. "I got held up at the office."

"No problem. My spaghetti isn't done yet."

"You're the chef tonight?"

"Yeah, but Tommie picked up a cake from that great new bakery, so you're safe for part of the evening." Pete laughed.

"I'm not worried," Jim assured him. Then he asked the question that had been on his mind all day. "Is Teresa here? I...haven't seen her in a while."

"Uh, neither had we," Pete said, staring at his brother as if wanting to say more.

Jim wondered what the odd look was for. But when he stepped into the family room and heard the words *Teresa* and *pregnant*, he knew.

Teresa Tyler was pregnant.

He stared at her in disbelief. If she was, it was early in her pregnancy; she wasn't showing much.

His mother didn't hesitate to state the obvious. "Teresa, you're pregnant! Congratulations!" she exclaimed. "I hadn't heard that you'd gotten married."

Teresa graciously accepted and returned the woman's hug. "Oh, hello, Evelyn. No, I haven't gotten married, but I am expecting. It's getting rather difficult to hide," Teresa responded with a smile, though her cheeks reddened like two ripe tomatoes.

"Well, where's the father of the baby?"

Jim knew his mother was embarrassing Teresa, with her inquisition but he was too interested in the answer to that question to interrupt.

Yes, just where was the father of her baby? He repeated to himself.

"The father and I aren't…together. I'll be raising my baby by myself." Teresa smiled again, but her shoulders held an obvious tension.

"And she'll have all the help she needs from us," said Ann Tyler, moving over to hug the youngest of her triplet daughters.

Feeling suddenly compelled to add his encouragement, perhaps to compensate for his mother's doubts, Jim said, "I'm sure she'll do fine." As if thanking him, Teresa glanced his way, met his eyes for a fleeting second, then locked her gaze on the iced tea she held in her hand.

Jim couldn't help himself from taking a long look at her. Her sleek blond hair was pulled back in her omnipresent braid, and she looked a little peaked. Whether from morning sickness or from the fifty questions, he didn't know. Against his better judgment he noticed her breasts, fuller now as they readied for the baby she'd soon nurse there. He stopped the mental picture before it started to take shape.

He no longer had a relationship with Teresa, he reminded himself. And that was the way he wanted it to be. Months ago, when his twin brother had first returned to Texas and met Tommie, the real estate agent helping relocate his Boston software firm and executives to Fort Worth, Pete had dragged him along to all kinds of business and social functions, the same functions to which Tommie had brought Teresa. Jim found himself dating Teresa to round out the numbers. But he'd opted out of that situation. Not because of Teresa, who was a beautiful and sweet woman, but because he wasn't comfortable double-dating with his twin. They'd tried that once before, with disastrous results.

He would do well to remember that, he told himself.

Evelyn, undeterred, was continuing to grill Teresa. "But how can you manage without a father for the baby?"

"Mom managed to raise the three of us without having a father in the house," Tommie pointed out.

"Oh, I forgot that," Evelyn said. "Probably because I always think of Joel as a part of the family."

Ann cleared her throat. "Well, actually, Joel and I have an announcement of our own, if you all don't mind."

Joel stepped closer to the slim blond woman, still beautiful in her fifties. His gaze sought out the triplets as he said, "Ann has agreed to m-marry me—if you have no objections."

All three of Ann's daughters jumped to their feet and hugged the newly engaged couple. "We're absolutely thrilled," Teresa said, a sentiment echoed by the others.

"I told him you'd be happy for us," Ann said, tears glistening in her eyes.

"Of course we are," Teresa managed through her smile. "And now my baby will have a granddad…if you don't mind, Joel."

The soft-spoken, gentle man stammered, "I—I'd be delighted!"

Jim stood quietly by while congratulations were offered, but his mind was not on Ann Tyler's upcoming nuptials. He was still back on the announcement of Teresa's pregnancy.

His eyes bored into her as he bluntly asked, "When is the baby due?" He couldn't get his brain to stop working, thinking, calculating.

Without looking at Jim, Teresa answered, "In about four months, give or take."

Four months… That put the conception somewhere around Pete and Tommie's wedding. He remembered the man who had escorted Teresa to the rehearsal dinner and the wedding, If he remembered correctly, he didn't like the guy much. He was awfully…handy. His hands were all over Teresa.

Before Jim could pursue the line of questioning, Tommie told everyone to take their seats for dinner. It was probably just as well. He needed the time to remind himself that this was none of his concern.

"And we have seats assigned, so be sure you're in the right place!" she added with a chuckle. "We found these cute place cards a couple of weeks ago. I couldn't wait to use them."

Jim found his name between Tabitha and Tommie at one end of the table. At the other end was Teresa, next to Pete. He couldn't have been any farther away from her. When his mother asked if she knew the sex of the baby yet, he had to lean forward to catch her answer.

"I'm going to the doctor on Wednesday for my sonogram. I can find out then," she said. "I haven't decided if I want to know yet."

Both her sisters protested. "Oh, no, we have to know so we can decorate the nursery in the right colors!" Tommie exclaimed.

"Yeah, and if it's a girl, we can buy some of those cute little outfits!" Tabitha added.

"Girls," Ann said quietly, "Teresa is in charge of her pregnancy. She gets to make the decisions."

Teresa laughed. "It's all right, Mom. They're probably right. I just haven't decided."

"How long are you going to teach?" Jim asked.

"Oh, um, I'm not teaching. I took a sabbatical."

"Then who's taking care of you?" Jim asked, forgetting to stay uninvolved at her shocking statement.

"I'm taking care of myself and my baby, Jim. And as much as I appreciate all your concerns," she said, addressing everyone at the table, "I'm managing just fine."

"Do you have any contact with the father?" Jim asked, his voice husky.

Teresa gritted her teeth and stared at Evelyn, who was seated across from her. "No, no contact!"

Pete reached over and patted her hand. "I think we've all got the message now, honey. No one will ask that question again." Since he accompanied his words with a determined stare at his brother, Jim backed down.

They lingered around the dinner table even after the dessert had been eaten, talking, exchanging news and discussing plans.

"Oh, by the way," Tommie asked in a lull in the conversation, "have you started decorating the nursery yet, Teresa?"

"Not yet. I've been using the other bedroom as a study. I'll have to move everything."

"Just remember that you mustn't do the painting."

"I think that's an old wives' tale. They have safe paint now," Teresa said.

"Maybe we should have a workday one Saturday and—"

"No!" Teresa's empathetic response interrupted Tommie. "Thank you, but I'll get it done in plenty of time, I promise."

Silence followed her response.

"I really do appreciate all the support, and I may make mistakes, but I want to learn the hard way, I guess." Teresa looked around the table, an anxious look on her face.

"I'm sure you'll manage," Jim said and received a warm smile in return. The first nice smile she'd awarded him since he'd told her he wouldn't be dating her anymore.

Good thing she wasn't a mind reader. Because as much as Teresa said she didn't need anyone, Jim knew she did. And he knew just where to look for help. He'd remembered the guy she'd been with at the wedding. His name had been Roger something, and he was a teacher at the same school where Teresa had taught kindergarten.

Jim intended to find the man. If nothing else, the creep would pay for having abandoned Teresa and his baby. Jim would see to that.

When the final dismissal bell rang on Monday at the elementary school where Teresa had taught kindergarten, the school erupted as students headed for happier pursuits.

Jim entered the office.

"May I help you, sir?" an elderly lady said from behind the counter.

"Yes, I hope so. This is embarrassing, but yesterday I ran out of gas and I was broke. This guy loaned me ten dollars and told me he was a teacher here. His first name was Roger, but I forgot his last name. I want to pay him back. Do you have anybody here by that name?" He used his most charming smile.

"Oh, that would have to be Roger Arnsby. He's the sweetest thing!" the grandmotherly woman said.

"Yes, of course. How could I have forgotten—Arnsby. What room is he in?"

"His room is one-oh-seven, just down the hall, but you'll have to sign in if you want to see him."

"Thank you, ma'am." Jim signed the visitor log and left the office. He quickly found the correct room. He rapped briefly on the door and stepped forward to face the man behind the desk.

He hurriedly stood and looked at Jim. "Can I help you?"

"Perhaps. We met at my brother's wedding in July."

"Oh, right, Teresa's sister's wedding," the teacher said with a relieved smile. "I knew you looked familiar."

"Oh, you remember Teresa?" Jim asked grimly.

The man frowned. "Of course I remember her. She's a friend."

"Seen her lately?"

"No, I called her in September to go get a cup of coffee. You know, touch base with her, but she was busy."

"Guess what she was busy with." Before Roger could answer, Jim continued, "She was throwing up because she's pregnant."

"Did you come here to tell me that?"

"I came here to tell you because she doesn't have a brother to inform you."

"Why would she need a— Wait just a minute! Are you implying she's pregnant with *my* baby?" Roger demanded, his voice rising close to hysteria.

"Glad to see you got my meaning. Now, I'm not sure Teresa wants you in her life, and that's her choice. But you owe her some financial support for your child."

"But I'm not the father of her child."

"Oh, really? How do you know?"

"I know because Teresa and I are friends. I never had sex with her."

"You seemed pretty hot and heavy at the rehearsal dinner and wedding," Jim reminded him.

"Yeah, because that's what she wanted. When I tried to continue the relationship because—because I was falling for her, she refused. Said she appreciated my help, but she wasn't ready for a relationship."

"Would you say that if she were standing here in front of you?"

"Yeah, I would. And I'd also want to share in my child's life, even if its mother still wasn't interested in me. But unless the ways to get pregnant have changed to include hand-holding, I'm not the dad. That's about as far as I've gone with Teresa."

Jim frowned ferociously and Roger took a step backward. "Ask Teresa if you don't believe me. I'm sure she didn't tell you that I was the father!"

"She didn't," Jim said with a growl. What the hell had gone on last summer? And why did she ask this bozo to slobber all over her at the rehearsal and wedding? It was as if she was trying to prove that she hadn't been hurt.

He turned, almost stumbling, and started out of the room. "Sorry," he muttered over his shoulder.

"Hey! Wait! Did you figure out who the father is?"

"I think so. Sorry I bothered you."

Jim got in his car and sat in the parking lot, trying to gather his thoughts.

Could it be?

He hadn't thought—

But she'd avoided him after he'd told her he wouldn't be seeing her anymore. That was for sure. Which meant he'd hurt her.

He hadn't intended to. Drumming his fingers on

the steering wheel, Jim thought about his reasons. As a teenager, he'd been embarrassed, humiliated by a girl who thought he was going to give her his senior ring. They had doubled with his brother and his girlfriend because his brother had asked him to. His senior year had been ruined because the girl had vilified him to everyone.

He'd vowed never to be caught in the same situation again.

Then Pete had come back home, met Tommie and the other two triplets. Somehow Jim had ended up dating Teresa. And he'd panicked as his mother kept talking about him marrying Teresa.

He'd felt he had to disassociate himself before any free choice was taken from him. He'd arranged to take Teresa to dinner one Friday night. Unfortunately, before he'd gotten up his nerve to tell her, she had acted out of character.

She'd seduced him.

Jim rubbed his face with his hands. That night had been wonderful…and horrible. He hadn't been strong enough to resist her, probably because he'd secretly wanted her all along. But after they'd made love, he'd still told her he wouldn't date her again.

Stupid of him.

There was no justification for what he'd done, except that he'd panicked. After having the most memorable sexual experience of his life, he'd rejected her.

But the most important question here was whether or not he was the father of her baby.

And that question had to be answered today!

Chapter Two

It only took one look from Teresa to change Jim's plans. He wasn't going to demand anything. Because he'd seen fear in her eyes.

"Jim! What are you doing here?" she'd asked.

What had he done to make her fear him? And if he demanded the truth now, when she already feared him, she'd never admit his role in her pregnancy.

"I wanted to come by and see you. Mind if I come in?"

"But why are you off work? It's too early for you—"

"I worked a lot of overtime last week. I thought I'd take off early today. And I wanted to offer my services to you."

"Your services? I don't need any accounting help."

He smiled, gently moving into her house as she backed away from him. "I know that. But I thought there might be some things I could do for you…like a brother."

"A brother?" Her voice wavered and Jim didn't know if she was going to laugh or cry.

"You know, lift things, move things. I'll pretend to be your brother while you're pregnant. You can call on me for anything."

They were still standing in the entryway. Jim didn't think he was going to get any farther into her home.

"Well, that's very thoughtful, Jim, but—"

Suddenly, a strange look came over her face and she felt her slightly protruding stomach.

"What is it? What's wrong? Come on, let's sit you down. This way," he said as he moved her into the living room toward the sofa.

"No, it's— I'm fine. I think I just felt the baby move—for the first time!" She beamed at him.

Jim wrapped his arms around her. "You scared me to death! That's good, isn't it? To feel the baby move?"

She eased herself out of his hold. "Yes, I'm sure it is. I'll ask the doctor Wednesday."

"What time is your appointment?"

"Two o'clock."

"What did it feel like?" Jim asked as he urged her to sit down.

She gave him a confused look. "What?"

"What did the movement feel like?"

"Oh. Kind of like a butterfly. Just a fluttering."

"Is that normal?"

"I think so. I haven't known anyone who's been pregnant. I can ask the doctor Wednesday." She frowned at him. "It was nice of you to stop by, Jim, but really, I'm fine."

"Good." He looked around the cozy room, one he remembered so well from his visits here last summer. "I like your living room. It's so comfortable. Hey!" he exclaimed. "Where's your television?"

"My television? I have a portable I keep in my bedroom."

"Is that the only one you have? What if you have someone over to watch television?"

"I don't."

"But the World Series starts this week. Aren't you going to watch it?"

"I don't know. Probably."

Jim got an idea. He knew just what he could do for Teresa, and he wanted to get onto it right away. "Well, if you don't need me, then…" He walked toward the door. "I'll see you Wednesday."

Teresa followed Jim to the door just in time to wave goodbye as he hurried to his car. What a strange visit. He wanted to be her brother? How would that work, when he was the father of her baby? Not that he knew that. Nor would he. She certainly wasn't going to tell him.

As she turned from the door, she couldn't help but think of the last time Jim Schofield was in her house. That summer night was forever emblazoned on her memory. It had certainly been different from today.

Then Jim wasn't looking to be her brother. Nor had she looked for fraternal affection from him. She'd tried her best that night to seduce him…and she'd succeeded. He'd given her the best night of her life.

Until he'd told her he didn't want to see her again.

Her memory jogged, and she suddenly remembered his most recent remark. He'd see her Wednesday. What did he mean by that?

Had Tommie planned something for her entire family again? Teresa didn't think sharing another meal with Jim was a good idea. She loved him, but he didn't love her, nor did he want anything to do with her…except as a brother.

And that was impossible.

When Teresa came out to get in her car Wednesday for her doctor's appointment, she remembered wondering what Jim had meant when he said he'd see her Wednesday.

Now she knew.

Jim's luxury car was parked in her driveway behind her own economy car. His window was rolled down and he sat behind the wheel.

She slowly walked over to him. "Jim? What are you doing here?"

"I'm here to take you to your doctor's appointment."

Teresa frowned. "Why?"

"Because I thought you sounded a little apprehensive talking about the appointment when I was here on Monday. I didn't think you should have to go through it alone."

Teresa fought back the sudden tears that filled her eyes. She turned away from Jim so he couldn't see them. "I'm afraid that's not possible, Jim. Everyone at the doctor's office would think you were the father. Rumors would start. Your mother would be appalled."

"My mother will survive. We'll tell everyone at the doctor's office that I'm your brother. It's almost true."

That brother thing again, she thought. Why did he torture her with that? "No. Please back out so I can leave." She turned and headed for her car.

Jim jumped out of his car and beat her to the door of her own. She thought he was being sweet and was going to open it for her. Instead, he leaned against it. "I'm not leaving."

"Jim, you're being unreasonable!"

"No, you're the one being unreasonable. I just want to help you."

"I don't need your help."

He stepped forward and put an arm around her shoulders. "You need someone's help, and I'm the only one here. If your sisters had shown up, I'd back off. But they didn't."

"I told them I'd be fine. There was no need for them to take off work."

"I agree. Come on, Teresa. Let me go with you."

"Okay, you can drive me there, but you have to stay in the waiting room while I'm examined."

"If that's what you want," he assured her as he opened his passenger door for her.

Once they were on their way, his gaze kept flitting to the side to catch a glimpse of her face. In a casual voice he said, "It seemed to me you were worried about what the sonogram might show. Am I right?"

"It's going to be fine, I'm sure."

He reached out and took her left hand in his, cradling it on his thigh. "Of course it is."

When Teresa tried to withdraw her hand, he held it fast. Finally she stopped fighting him. After all, no one else could see, and it did give her some extra courage at the moment—and she needed that.

When they reached the doctor's office, Teresa signed in, then sat down beside Jim. "It shouldn't take too long. I'll be his first patient after lunch."

"That's good. Does it embarrass you to be seen by a man?"

When she stared at him, he clarified. "I mean, the doctor is a man, isn't he?"

"Well, yes, but…you know, the nurses drape me. He'll only see my stomach today."

"I've seen your stomach before, Teresa," he whispered, watching her closely.

She turned a bright red. "Not like it is now."

"Come on, Teresa, let me come in with you. I've never seen a sonogram before."

"I—I don't—"

"Miss Tyler?" the nurse called from the just-opened door.

Jim followed Teresa to the door. "I want to come in when the doctor does the sonogram. She'll be properly draped, won't she?"

"Yes, of course. But that decision is Miss Tyler's, unless you're the father?"

Jim looked from the nurse to Teresa, and she could feel her heart start to race. How was she supposed to answer that?

In Jim's expression she could see how much she wanted to come in, to be a witness to the first sight of her baby. Their baby. Even though she couldn't tell him he was going to be a father, she couldn't in all good conscience deny him this opportunity. She swallowed the fear she tasted in her mouth and said to the nurse, "He's just a good friend, but it's okay with me if he comes in for the sonogram." Then, without a glance in his direction, she headed down the hallway toward the examination rooms.

"All right, Miss Tyler, I'll let the doctor know you're ready. Are you excited?"

Teresa rubbed her damp hands on the white cloths covering her naked body as she lay on the exam table. "Yes…and a little apprehensive."

The nurse reassured her. "I'm sure you have nothing to worry about. Shall I show your friend in now?"

"Oh, I—I—"

Before she could complete her thought, the nurse reminded her, "You did say he could come in, didn't you?"

"Yes, but—"

"It will make you feel better to have him with you. I'll go get him."

She whisked out of the room, leaving Teresa even

more alarmed than before. What if there was something wrong with her baby? The nurse said she'd gained quite a bit of weight, and the doctor might be concerned.

Now that she thought of it, she didn't think it would be good for Jim to hang around. She might weaken and tell him it was his child. But she'd promised herself she wouldn't do that. She didn't want a man who had to be trapped. He should know about his child. But not now. Later, when she wasn't pregnant.

The door opened and Jim came in smiling at her. "I appreciate you letting me come in, honey."

Teresa tried to smile at him, but she didn't quite pull it off.

He immediately came to her side and took her hand in his, as he had in the car. The warmth his hand provided began to seep through her. She would've been greatly embarrassed if his gaze had not remained on her face. But it did.

"It will be all right," Jim promised.

She didn't try to respond because the door opened again to allow Dr. Benson to enter, followed by the nurse.

"Mr. Schofield, if you'll move to the other side of Miss Tyler, it will make our job easier," the nurse assured him, smiling at him.

Teresa wondered if she was flirting with Jim. He was an attractive man, tall, muscular with dark hair and the most beautiful hazel eyes she'd ever seen. She could understand why the young nurse would be interested. After all, hadn't he stolen her own heart when he wasn't even trying. Foolish her.

The doctor began chatting about her pregnancy, and Teresa was forced to take her mind off Jim. But he continued to hold her hand.

"You've gained a couple more pounds than I expected, my dear. Have you been doing a lot of munching between meals? You have to watch that. We want a healthy baby, you know."

"Yes, doctor," Teresa said, biting her bottom lip.

He must've seen her uneasiness. "Well, now, I'm sure you'll be careful. The nurse is going to put some petroleum jelly on your stomach so we can get a picture of your baby."

Teresa clutched Jim's hand as if it were a lifeline. She didn't bother looking at him to make sure he wasn't staring in disgust at her stomach. Instead she kept her eyes on the nurse's movement. The jelly felt a little cold and a bit slimey. But she so badly wanted to see her baby and make sure it was all right.

"Now I'm going to press down on your stomach," Dr. Benson said. "It may be a little uncomfortable, but it will ensure a good picture. You watch the monitor."

Teresa fastened her eyes on the small screen. When the picture came through, they all watched closely.

"Well, well, well," the doctor said a few moments later, beaming a broad smile at Teresa. "I see now why you picked up the extra pounds. I should've expected this. After all, you *are* a triplet."

Good thing she was lying down, or the news might have knocked her to her back. Was he saying what she thought he was? "Dr. Benson, does this mean… Am I having…"

He nodded his head. "Twins."

Not one baby, but two? What Tommie had feared about her relationship with Pete—a multiple birth— had come true for her.

She sobered suddenly as a fearsome thought hit home. Would Jim think he was the father? After all, he was a twin. She tried to remove her hand from his. After getting this profound news, she couldn't face another pronouncement right now.

Thankfully she heard the doctor ask, "Do you want to know the sex of your babies?"

Jim squeezed her hand. She didn't know what that meant, but she'd made her decision before she arrived at the doctor's office. "Yes, I do."

The doctor beamed down at her. "You're having twin boys, my dear. Your life is going to be very busy."

"Yes," Teresa agreed, avoiding Jim's gaze. Twin boys. She didn't know anything about boys. No, she corrected herself, that wasn't true. She had about fifteen of them every year in her kindergarten class. But sons? She was having two sons?

As if sensing how overwhelmed she was, the kindly sexagenarian doctor patted her hump. "Now, I'm going to go to my office. After the nurse cleans you up and you get dressed, she'll show you to my office and we'll have a little talk. I can answer any questions you might have."

"Thank you, doctor." She waited for the nurse to take Jim back to the waiting room.

"Mr. Schofield, is it? You want to wait in my office for Teresa?" the doctor asked.

Teresa wanted to scream no. Jim had no business being in the consultation with them.

However, before she could protest, he bent over and kissed her forehead and accepted the doctor's invitation.

"So, the babies are all right?" Jim asked Dr. Benson as he followed him into the office. "And Teresa?"

"All three are in perfect shape." The doctor sat in his leather chair and smoothed his tie over his chest. "Mr. Schofield, if you don't mind my asking, how are you related to this situation?"

"I'm Teresa's sister's husband's brother," Jim said. "I came with her as a friend, sort of as her brother."

The doctor nodded his head, and began jotting some notes in a file. He didn't look up as he spoke. "I think under the circumstances we'd better wait until Teresa comes in. But I hope you will continue to offer her support. It won't be easy to raise two little boys by herself."

"I'm a twin myself," Jim said. At that, the doctor picked up his head, fully attentive. Jim knew what the man was thinking. A mother who was a triplet—and a father who was a twin? But Jim revealed nothing. He had no right to divulge the truth. Only Teresa could do that.

"Really?" Dr. Benson intoned, trying for mildly interested. "Then you'll be a lot of help."

Jim wanted that responsibility. Though he'd never

pictured himself married, he was willing to take that leap so that he could be involved in his sons' lives. He'd never deny his kids. He'd also never regret them. Though this complicated situation was created out of his own stupidity, Jim vowed to do what was right.

The door opened and Teresa, again dressed in a turquoise dress that made her blue eyes look huge, stepped into the office.

"Come in, my dear. I'm so pleased with your pregnancy. Now, do you have any questions?"

Teresa stared first at the doctor and then at Jim.

Before she could speak, Jim reminded her, "Don't you want to ask about the baby, I mean babies, moving?"

"You felt the babies moving?" Dr. Benson asked.

"I felt what I would describe as a flutter. It worried me," she admitted.

"That's a good sign. Perfectly normal. Now, I want you to continue your normal activities, but don't push yourself. A nap every day would be good. Pamper yourself, but don't overeat."

"Yes, doctor."

"Do you have any other questions?"

"I—I can't think of any others," she said faintly.

"Good. But you call if you're worried about something. I think the best thing for your babies is to have a happy mom. You should be spoiled and cared for. Mr. Schofield has promised—as your brother, sort of—to be sure you're cared for. I'm holding him to his promise."

"No! He isn't my— It's not his responsibility. I can take care of myself!"

"That's exactly what I mean," the doctor said as Teresa jumped from her chair. "It's not good for the babies or for you to get agitated."

Teresa sank back into her chair, assisted by Jim, and took deep breaths. "I'm sorry. I'll be careful. My sisters will check in on me. That will be sufficient."

In a fatherly manner, the doctor said, "My dear, you should never turn down a friend. We all need any help we can get."

Jim watched Teresa's jaw tighten, just as it had when he'd asked who was the father of her babies. "She'll be careful, doctor. She loves children."

"Good." He stood and held out his hand first to Teresa and then to Jim. "Let me know if you have any questions."

Teresa nodded and headed out of his office, not waiting for Jim. He sighed but caught up with her. "Teresa, are you mad at me?"

"Yes, I am. You had no right to talk to my doctor. You're poking your nose in where it doesn't belong."

"We didn't discuss anything except that I'm a twin. Unlike you, he didn't feel I was being nosy." About the time he finished that statement, he noticed she was carefully carrying a paper. "What's that?"

A warm flush covered her cheeks. "A copy of the sonogram. The nurse printed it out for me."

Jim hadn't realized Teresa would have a picture. "May I see?"

"You were there, Jim."

"I know, but…it all went by so fast."

They had reached his car and he held open the door for her. Then he circled the car to get behind the wheel. Without a word, Teresa handed over the sonogram picture.

Jim noted that his hands were shaking as he took the picture of his sons. There they were. Two baby boys. "Dear God, Teresa, this is so wonderful. You might have preferred triplets, but…" His voice trailed off as he looked at the two small shapes.

"No. I'll have to struggle to manage with two boys. Three would do me in," she said with a small smile.

"And now, more than ever, I want to help you. After all, I'm a male twin. I can give you advice, help you deal with…anything."

She closed her eyes and laid her head against the headrest. "I don't need any help, Jim. Please take me home."

He carefully put the picture back in her lap and started the car. "Are you going to show your sisters the picture?" he asked.

"Probably, the next time I see them."

"But—"

"Jim, these are my babies and my decision. They don't have to know immediately. The babies and I aren't going anywhere!"

Jim pressed his lips together to stop himself from arguing with her. That was the last thing she needed. It would make her blood pressure go up.

When they reached her house, she got out of the car before he could reach her door. As she started for her house, he said, "You unlock the door. I'm going to get something out of the trunk."

Teresa turned around to stare at him. "What? I don't need anything."

"I'll be right there." He took a large flat box out of the car and started toward her.

Teresa stared at the box, unable to figure out what it could be. Then she saw the writing on it. That couldn't be a television.

Jim hefted the box through the door while she held it open. Then she followed him into the living room.

"Jim, what is that? What are you doing?"

"I thought I'd loan you a television for your living room, so you can rest."

"I have a television in my bedroom. I can rest there. Besides, that's too flat for a television."

"It's a new—uh, relatively new plasma television. And it has that new picture. I'll just hang it on the wall." He put down the box and looked around. "May I take down this picture?"

"Jim, I don't need a television. And I like that painting."

"Sit down and take deep breaths, Teresa. Let me just show you how this will work." He removed the picture and went about hanging the TV in its place. A while later he moved back and picked up the remote control. A blast of noise came out of the flat television, cheering as the camera panned the audience at a baseball game.

"The game's on already?" Teresa asked, immediately captured by the big screen and sharp clarity.

"Yeah. It just started."

Teresa reluctantly turned from the television to look at Jim. "I really don't need this television. I don't want to take it away from you."

"The doctor said you should be pampered," Jim reminded her. "I'm just following his directions. Mind if I stay and watch the game?"

Chapter Three

Jim was opening the door of his condo when his phone rang. Catching it on an umpteenth ring, he barked a hello.

"Where have you been, Jim?" It was his mother. "I've tried to reach you all evening."

Actually, he'd had a pleasant afternoon and evening with Teresa, but he wasn't about to tell his mother that. She'd read more into it than there was. After the game he'd ordered in some Chinese food, which they ate while they discussed safe topics like baseball strategy. Then on his way home he'd stopped at a coffee shop and drank coffee he hadn't really wanted because he was afraid of spending time alone with his thoughts.

But all he told his mother was "I was out, Mom. Is something wrong?"

"Can't a mother call her son without there being a reason?"

Jim stifled a laugh. Yeah, like that ever happened. "Well, thanks for calling. How are you?"

"I've decided I need to have the house repainted. Whom should I call?"

At ten o'clock at night she wanted him to thumb through the Yellow Pages? He said, "I don't think your house needs painting. Didn't you just have it done last year?"

"Yes, but I want to update it. Maybe I'll just have the interior done. I could do one room in blue, one in pale yellow…oh, and I saw a red room on one of those home-improvement shows. It looked so chic!"

"Okay, if that's what you want, Mom. Maybe hire a decorator to advise you."

"A decorator? Why, that's a wonderful idea. I could ask Teresa and Tommie. They did such a good job on Pete's new house. I'll invite them to lunch and ask their advice. Thank you, dear. I knew you'd know what to do. That's why I rely on you so much, Jim."

Jim could practically see her beaming through the phone. "I love you, too, Mom."

When his mother hung up, he phoned Tommie himself. But for another reason altogether. It was late, but he didn't want to waste one more minute putting into action the plan he'd come up with tonight.

When Pete answered, Jim asked, "Is Tommie awake?"

"Yeah, Jim…but what do you want her for?"

"I'm not hitting on your wife, bro. I want her to find me a house. And I have to warn her about Mom."

"What about Mom?" Pete asked. "And what's this about a home?"

"I can't tell you over the phone. Besides… Hell, I don't know if I should tell you at all."

"Look, we're still up. Why don't you come over and Tommie will make a pot of decaf, okay?"

"All right, if you're sure."

Jim stopped at the grocery store and bought a package of brownies, as a peace offering. It might take a lot more than chocolate when he faced Tommie.

Pete must've been watching for him because he opened the door as Jim reached the porch. "Come on in. You've certainly stirred our curiosity."

"I didn't mean to sound so mysterious," Jim said. He followed Pete to the kitchen where Tommie had put on the coffee and set out three mugs. Jim slid the box of brownies toward her. "I hope you like these."

"Oh, I love them, and so do my hips."

Jim drew a deep breath after he was seated. "Teresa went to the doctor today."

Tommie exclaimed, "Oh, I forgot about that. I need to call her." She moved toward the phone.

"She'll be asleep," Jim pointed out.

Tommie automatically looked at her watch. "You could be right. I'll call her in the— Wait a minute. How do you know so much about Teresa?"

"I went with her to the doctor's office."

Pete stared at his brother. "Why?"

Jim swallowed. "I—I thought she was apprehensive about the sonogram, so I went with her."

"She agreed to that? She told me I couldn't come with her, that she could manage on her own."

"She wasn't thrilled about having me come along, but I did, and she let me come in while they did the sonogram."

"Wait," Tommie ordered. She poured the coffee and carried the mugs to the table. After she sat down, she looked at Jim. "She agreed to your staying in the room with her while they did the sonogram?"

"Yes. She felt the baby move on Monday for the first time and it made her a little nervous."

"But everything was all right?" Tommie asked urgently, leaning forward.

"Yes." Jim stopped, trying to think what he should say. Finally, he blurted out, "She's having twin boys."

Excitement lit up Tommie's face for a moment. Then she said, "Don't you think you should've let Teresa tell us?"

Pete took Tommie's hand. "I think my brother has more to tell us, honey."

Tommie looked from her husband's face to Jim's. "What?"

"I know who the father is," Jim confessed, staring at his coffee.

Pete said nothing, but Tommie demanded to know at once.

Jim raised his gaze to the woman, prepared to take his medicine. "Tommie, I'm the father of Teresa's babies."

Tommie stared at him. Then in a low voice, she said, "You bastard! You get my baby sister pregnant and then abandon her? How dare you!"

"I didn't know she was pregnant. I mean, not until Saturday night. I only figured out I was the daddy on Monday. I thought it was the guy at her school. The one that was all over her at the rehearsal dinner and the wedding. I confronted him. But it wasn't him. He said Teresa asked him to act that way for those two events, then refused to see him again."

"Why would she do that?" Tommie asked.

"Because she wanted to make sure no one would know that I'd hurt her. We…we had sex before I told her I couldn't date her anymore because of what had happened to me before."

Pete stared at his brother this time. "Don't you think that's a little cold?"

"Yes, damn it, I do. But I wasn't prepared— She didn't— I panicked."

"Couldn't you have panicked *before* you made love to her?" Tommie asked in an icy voice.

"I don't blame you if you don't believe me, Tommie, but she took me by surprise. I was trying to get my nerve up to tell her my decision. We went back to her house and—and she seduced me."

"Teresa? No, I don't believe you!" Tommie exclaimed.

"That is a little far-fetched, bro," Pete agreed.

"I know. That's why I was totally unprepared. She's beautiful and sweet and—and that's the last thing I thought she would do. And I was weak. I took what she offered."

There was silence around the table for several minutes. Then Tommie said, "Now what?"

"I'm willing to marry her. I'm certainly not going to ignore my responsibilities. And I want to play a role in my sons' lives. But I'm afraid she'll turn me down and refuse to let me have anything to do with the pregnancy if I confront her now."

"Do you love her?" Tommie asked sharply.

"I respect her, and I like her, too. I can't say I'm in love with her," he said, being as honest as he could.

Tommie jumped up from her chair before her husband could stop her and started pacing the floor, her arms wrapped around her middle.

"Tommie?" Pete called softly.

She spun around and glared at him. "What?"

"What are you thinking?"

"I'm thinking about poor Teresa. She won't accept an offer like that, based on him wanting his sons and *agreeing* to take Teresa, too. And I don't want her to. I want her to have what we have, a marriage filled with love."

Jim muttered, "I'm trying to be honest."

"What do you want Jim to do?" Pete asked his wife.

"That's Teresa's decision," Tommie finally said, tears in her eyes.

"That's why I want you to look for a house for me," Jim put in. "It will be a place for Teresa and the boys. I'll be there if she wants, or I'll stay in the condo. But something close to my condo and you two, so she won't feel alone. Her house is nice, but the neighborhood is a little run-down. I want her safe."

"You're going to buy a house?" Pete asked.

"I'm starting a family. It will need to be single-story so if I convince Teresa to move in before the boys are born, it won't be a problem for her. I need at least three bedrooms, preferably four, and a big backyard where they can play."

Tommie came back to the table and sat down. "You're going to ask Teresa to move into this house whether she marries you or not?"

"That's my plan. I intend to provide for my family."

"All right. I'll find you a house—you and Teresa. Does she get any say about which house?"

"She can have as much say as she wants. But I'd rather you didn't tell her I know the babies are mine just yet."

"When are you going to tell her?" Tommie asked.

Jim took a gulp of the coffee. That was certainly the million-dollar question.

When Teresa awoke the next morning, she felt terribly guilty. She'd allowed Jim to go to the doctor's office and see the sonogram. Then she'd put up no resistance to his staying to watch the baseball game.

He'd ordered in food for them, saying he wanted to be sure she ate a good meal. After all, she was eating for three now. His consideration was sweet. Too sweet. She wasn't going to be caught believing in a fantasy world again.

After all, that was why she was in the situation she

was now, pregnant and alone. That night last summer she'd believed that Jim's actions had meant he loved her. But that wasn't true. He'd lusted after her. He'd made exquisite love to her. Then he'd told her he couldn't date her again. She'd accepted his statement. It had broken her heart, but she hadn't realized at the time that he'd ruined her life.

No! She wouldn't believe that her babies were a bad thing. She loved them already. She'd known fairly early that she was pregnant. She hadn't been able to pretend she wasn't since she threw up every morning. Yet, even then she'd hoped he would come back to her. She couldn't believe he'd been untouched by their lovemaking. But obviously he had.

Now, when she was alone, she imagined his arms around her, holding her safe. Her dream of a family hadn't come out as she'd planned it. His returning now, offering comfort but not love, was more dangerous than making love to her. She was weaker, hungrier now, but for her boys' sake, she had to be strong.

Which made her behavior last night deplorable. She'd fallen asleep in his arms while watching the ball game.

"How dumb can you be?" she demanded of herself as she brushed her teeth. Today the television must be returned. After she accomplished that, she'd send him on his way. These were *her* babies. After they were born, she'd tell Jim they were also his children. They could set up visitation rights after the boys were a year old.

But she didn't want to.

She checked her watch. It was almost nine o'clock. She was sure both her sisters were at work. Tabitha couldn't come to the phone with classes on-going. But she could tell Tommie her good news.

When her sister answered the phone, she said, "Tommie, it's Teresa. I wanted to tell you my news."

"What news?"

"I'm having twin boys," she said quietly.

Silence.

"I'm excited about it, Tommie. I thought you would be, too."

"But you're all alone, Teresa. I worry about you. Are you all right?"

"I'm fine, big sis. Don't be a worrywart. This means you and Tabitha won't have to fight over one baby. There will be one for each of you to hold."

"That's true. I hadn't thought of that. That's wonderful news, Teresa. I'm so happy for you."

"Thanks, sis. I won't keep you. I know you have lots of work to do."

"Maybe I'll take you out to lunch today. Would that be all right?"

"I'd love it, if you have time."

"Of course I do. I'll pick you up at eleven forty-five."

"Why don't you tell me where to meet you and I'll drive myself. It will give us more time to visit before you have to go back to work."

"Are you sure you can?"

"Tommie, I'm not bedridden. I can still drive."

"Okay, if you're sure." She picked a restaurant and gave Teresa directions.

* * *

Teresa enjoyed lunching out with her sister. Maybe she'd stayed home too much in the past weeks, though she'd certainly enjoyed working on her book. Still, she should get out a little more. It lifted her spirits.

After she expressed those thoughts to her sister, Tommie invited her to look at houses with her for the afternoon. "There are several new listings I need to check out. It'll be fun."

"Oh, I'd love that."

Tommie drove them both in her car.

"Where are the houses we're going to visit?"

"They're all in our neighborhood," Tommie said casually.

"Are they all new? I didn't realize they were building that many new homes."

"A couple are brand-new. This first one we're going to visit was built three years ago. The couple who owns it is moving to Cincinnati because of the husband's job transfer. The wife is just sick about it. She said she'd worked hard to make the house absolutely perfect. If what she says is true, I don't think it will last long."

"You think people like those kind better than new?"

"Think about it. They won't have to landscape, put up fences or anything, but it's in good condition."

"I hadn't thought of that."

Tommie stopped her car in front of a beautiful home. "Well, it certainly has curb appeal."

"This is the house? Oh, look at her beautiful flowers."

"I know. It makes the house inviting, doesn't it?"

They walked up to the door together.

When the lady of the house answered, she stared at them.

"I'm Tommie Schofield, Mrs. Jenkins. This is my sister Teresa. I called earlier about previewing your house this afternoon."

"Of course, come in. I was just thrown because you two look so much alike."

"We're used to the reaction. We're actually triplets, but my other sister is teaching."

"Oh my, triplets. That's wonderful. We're expecting our second child in seven months."

The woman didn't look pregnant except for a glow when she talked about her child. Teresa understood.

They walked through the house with their hostess. She pointed out the improvements she'd made in the kitchen, which looked perfect to both sisters, with a connected breakfast room with a bow window that looked out on a gorgeous backyard. There were three or four trees, one which shaded the back patio in the afternoons.

"This is beautiful," Teresa said with a sigh, picturing her little boys running and playing in the lush greenness. She didn't have much of a yard at home.

When they finished touring the house, they both shook the lady's hand and thanked her for letting them look at it. Tommie told her she had a specific buyer in mind. Would she mind if they came that evening if the buyer was free?

"Why no, I'd be delighted. It's painful to sell the

house, but the sooner the better. I want to get my new house in Cincinnati and work on it before I get too big."

After they got in the car, Teresa asked, "Who is the new client?"

"Oh, he's kin to someone who bought a house from me earlier. He called yesterday, and I think this house would be perfect."

"Are we going to look at any others?"

"There are a couple of new ones, if you have time."

"Sure, I'll enjoy it."

"Just be sure to let me know if you start getting tired."

After looking at the two new houses, Teresa confessed that she was tired. "I think I'm missing my afternoon nap."

"It's not a problem, Teresa. Do you feel up to driving home, or shall I—"

"Of course I can drive home. Oh, and I have something in my trunk that I'd like you to take to your house. Then the next time Jim is over, you can give it to him."

Tommie stared at her until she had to pay attention to her driving. "What is it?"

"A television."

"A television? He gave you a television? Why?"

"He thought I needed a big TV in my living room, so he loaned one to me."

"And you carried it to your car? Teresa, you can't do that!"

"I had lots of help. Wait until you see it. It's one of those plasma TVs. I think he must have more than one. But I don't need it and he might, so I'm returning it."

"He gave it to you yesterday?"

"Yes."

"Couldn't you just keep it until he comes back?"

Teresa's chin went up. "I don't want him to come back. He acts as though he's responsible for me, and he's not." With a soft grin, she added, "I already have two sisters who take care of me."

"You certainly do," Tommie assured her. "Okay, I'll take the television."

When they reached Teresa's car, they carefully transferred the big box to Tommie's car trunk. Then, as they said goodbye, Tommie asked, "The first house is the one you liked best, isn't it?"

"Oh, yes. The landscaping was wonderful, but the house was great, too. The kitchen and breakfast room in particular."

"Yes, and it has four bedrooms, too."

"The buyer you have in mind wants four bedrooms? He must have a big family," Teresa said with a smile. "That backyard looked wonderful for kids." She unconsciously put her hand to her stomach, thinking about her children.

"Okay. I just wanted a second opinion." She leaned over and kissed her sister goodbye. "Drive carefully."

"I will. And I enjoyed our day. Thanks, Tommie."

"Me, too. Talk to you soon," she promised as she got back in her car. But she didn't drive away until she saw Teresa get in her car and lock the doors.

Tommie used that time to call Jim. "I've found the house for you."

"Already? Are you sure?"

"Teresa and I saw it today, and I can show it to you this afternoon or evening. Do you have time?"

"Yes, if Teresa liked it. You didn't tell her, did you?"

"No. I just invited her to look at a few houses with me, for a second opinion. She loved it. I think you will, too."

"Give me half an hour and I'll meet you there. What's the address?"

Tommie relayed the information to him. Then she put her car in gear, waved goodbye to her sister and drove away. When she stopped at a red light, she dialed the owners and asked if she could show the house in half an hour.

Once that was set up, she ran by her office. Then she met Jim outside the lovely home.

"Well, it looks good so far," he said as he got out of his car.

"It looks just as good on the inside. This couple takes good care of the home."

"Why are they selling?"

"Her husband's been transferred to Cincinnati."

"Poor guy," Jim said.

"Yes, but it can be fortunate for you."

Tommie showed Jim through the house, and he was as impressed as Teresa had been earlier over the kitchen and breakfast area and the huge backyard.

"You're right, Tommie," Jim said. "This house is perfect. And you're sure Teresa liked it?"

"It was her favorite."

"Then, I think this is it. Can we write up an offer now?"

"Of course. Let's go back to my office."

An hour later, Tommie had a signed offer. She contacted the agent who'd listed the house and promised to bring the contract over at once.

Then she and Jim walked down to the parking lot.

"I have something for you," she said as they stepped out of the building.

"You do?" Jim asked in surprise.

"Yes. Teresa asked me to give you back the television. She thought you might need it, and she didn't."

"I bought it especially for her. I just told her I was loaning it to her, so she'd keep it." Jim looked upset.

"I'm afraid Teresa isn't one to accept charity. Are you sure you want to buy the house? She may not accept that gift either."

"I have to try, Tommie. I want my boys to be happy."

Tommie sighed. He wasn't going to be able to convince Teresa, she was pretty sure. What would he do then?

Chapter Four

After her nap, Teresa called her mother and Tabitha to tell them her good news. Tabitha insisted on treating her to dinner to celebrate.

"If I don't watch out, Dr. Benson will have to weigh me on a truck scale pretty soon." But Teresa could never say no to her sister.

When Tabitha picked her up, they discussed her babies all the way to the restaurant. Once they were seated, though, Teresa changed the subject, asking about her sister's new video.

"It's going so well! The school districts in Texas are eating it up. We're going to advertise nationwide next week."

"That's wonderful. You're going to end up richer than Tommie. I'll admit I never thought that would happen."

"Me, neither," Tabitha said with a giggle.

"Are you thinking about quitting teaching?"

"I don't know. I'm almost afraid to. I might lose touch with the teenagers. Then I couldn't make videos they like."

"I don't think that will happen. Besides, you'll have two nephews. They'll keep you in touch."

"True. Maybe I can do a video of exercises for children in daycare programs."

"That's not a bad idea," Teresa agreed with a smile.

After they were silent for several minutes, Tabitha asked, "Are you happy, Teresa?"

"Actually, I am. I'd be happier if I wasn't alone, but I'm fortunate to have such great sisters and Mother and Joel. He's promised to spend time with the boys."

"There's no chance you'll make up with their daddy?"

Teresa swallowed and then shook her head.

"Have you told him you're having twins?"

Again Teresa shook her head.

"But you have to tell him. It wouldn't be fair not to tell him."

Teresa chose her words carefully. "I'll make sure he knows. It's not going to matter."

"What if he wants to play a role in the boys' lives?"

"I wouldn't try to keep them from their daddy, unless he was harming them. But maybe he'll have other interests."

"And will you?"

Teresa stared at her sister. "What do you mean by that?"

"Are you in love with the man? Or will you be able to move on to someone else?"

"Tabitha, I'm going to be too busy for a few years even to think about anyone else."

"Like Mom? Are you going to wait until your sons are out of college and on their own before you take care of yourself?"

"It didn't hurt Mom," Teresa said firmly.

"Don't you think she wishes now she'd looked for Joel earlier?"

Teresa shrugged. "Things happen in their own time, sis. She might not have found Joel."

"I know. But I'm afraid you're hung up on the man who—who betrayed you."

"How about I promise to keep my eyes open? When I have time to look up."

That satisfied Tabitha for a while, and they ate quietly until she brought up another topic Teresa had been considering lately.

"Have you figured out what to name them?"

"I've thought about it a little. I'd like to name one of them Thomas, after Dad. I think that would please Mom."

Tabitha nodded. "That's a wonderful idea. But what about the other one?"

"I don't know. I have plenty of time yet to make up my mind. I may even wait until I see them. With some babies, you just know certain names won't fit their personalities."

Truthfully, she'd been wondering what Jim's father's name was, thinking it'd be nice and symmetrical to name the boys after their grandfathers. But she kept the thought to herself.

After dinner, when Tabitha dropped her off at home, she warned her to lock her door and be careful. "I think you should move into a nicer neighborhood. Tommie and I could—"

"No, my neighborhood is fine. I'll manage." She smiled at her anxious sister. "Thank you for dinner. It was wonderful."

When she entered her house, after having locked her door, she saw that the light on her answering machine was blinking furiously. She pressed the button, expecting to hear Tommie's voice. Instead, it was Jim.

"Teresa, I'm disappointed you returned the television. I wanted you to enjoy it. Give me a call when you get in. We need to talk."

Teresa erased the message and made no attempt to call Jim. She told herself it was too late, though it was only a little after nine. Frankly she just couldn't deal with Jim tonight.

When the phone rang ten minutes later, she thought it might be Jim, but the caller ID indicated it was Evelyn Schofield.

"Hello?"

"I'm glad I got you, dear. You hadn't gone to bed, had you?"

"No, Evelyn. How are you?"

"I'm fine. But I'm calling to ask a favor."

"I'll be glad to help you if I can."

"I'm thinking about doing some painting and re-decorating. I wondered if you could come to lunch tomorrow and help me choose the best colors."

"I'm not an expert, Evelyn, but I'll be glad to look at some colors with you. You don't have to feed me lunch."

"Nonsense, I'm delighted. Can you come about eleven-thirty?"

"Yes. Do you have paint samples for us to look at?"

"How smart of you to think of that. I'll ask Jim to get some for me."

"No, there's no need to bother Jim. I can pick up some on the way over."

"Oh, you are such a dear. That would be lovely. I'll see you tomorrow, then."

She'd no sooner hung up and stripped off her clothes to take a shower than the phone rang again. She grabbed it and wrapped a towel around herself at the same time. The voice on the other end made her regret not checking the caller I.D.

"Hello, Teresa. I take it you didn't get my message?"

Teresa backed up and sat down on the bed. "I did, but I was tired. I thought I'd call you tomorrow." She was lying, but he didn't have to know that.

"I wouldn't have known you were home, but my mother called to tell me how wonderful you are."

"Your mother is very generous," Teresa said softly.

"Yeah. I was trying to be generous when I brought over the television."

Teresa paused before she said, "I appreciated your

generosity, but I really don't watch that much TV. There was no reason for you to give up one of yours for me."

He was the one who paused then. Finally, he said, "Teresa, I know."

"You know what?"

"I know I'm the one who got you pregnant."

Every nerve ending in her body went on red alert. Her heart started racing and her mouth went bone-dry. She tried to speak, but it was as if the synapses from her brain to her mouth got jammed up. What would she say anyway? Deny it? Deflect it? Accept the inevitable?

Finally, she managed to find her voice. "I don't know how you could know that. You don't know whether I've slept with anyone else since then." She was proud of herself for keeping the panic out of her tone.

"I know you didn't sleep with Roger."

Teresa stared at the phone, as if it were inhabited by a monster. How did he know that? Unless he…

"*Have* you slept with anyone else?" he asked, his voice getting louder and more impatient.

She clenched her teeth and said, "Who I've slept with is none of your business." And to punctuate the sentence, she slammed the phone in his ear.

Jim had made a mistake.

A big one.

But he'd been so frustrated that she'd returned the TV. In so doing, she'd made it clear to him that she wanted nothing to do with him.

They'd had such a nice evening on Wednesday, watching the game, talking. Heck, she'd even fallen asleep on his shoulder. By that time he'd convinced himself that marrying Teresa would be all right.

Then she'd thrown the TV back in his face—and denied he was the daddy.

She was so damn frustrating. No matter how he tried, he couldn't figure her out. As an accountant, he was used to numbers adding up, making sense. From whatever angle you looked at it, two plus two always made four. Why couldn't Teresa be more like the numbers he juggled all day?

Was it pregnancy hormones? He remembered another accountant at the office last year who'd been highly temperamental when she was expecting her daughter. Maybe that was it.

Jim paced as he thought. He damn near wore a hole through his carpet trying to find a way to deal with Teresa. A way to convince her to share their babies with him.

By sunup, he'd at least come up with a partial plan. But, of all people, he needed his mother.

Teresa was actually looking forward to lunch with Evelyn. Teresa and Tommie had gotten to know the older woman quite well when they'd worked on Pete's house last summer. Besides, Teresa loved decorating.

On the way there she stopped by a paint store and picked up the samples she'd promised to get. Armed with the latest in trendy choices, she couldn't wait to show Evelyn the array of selection…until she pulled up in front of the woman's lovely home and spotted Jim's car in the driveway.

Why was he there?

She wanted to keep right on driving. Take her paint chips and run. But she'd promised Evelyn. Maybe, she told herself, Jim had left his car there for some reason.

Drawing a deep breath, she parked and went to the front door.

Evelyn opened the door, all smiles. "Teresa. I'm so glad you're here."

Teresa looked past the woman, into the hall. No sign of Jim.

She smiled back and followed Evelyn into her living room. "Your house is so beautiful. I don't see anything that needs redoing."

"Perhaps not, dear. But it's time for a change."

Teresa was about to show Evelyn some color choices when she heard footsteps on the stairs. Not turning around, she asked, "Is someone here?"

"Why, yes. Jim asked to come to lunch today, too. And," she added with a wink, "I don't think he's here to see me."

Teresa spun around. "Jim! I didn't know you would be here."

"I thought I'd have lunch with you and Mother. It's a slow day at work." He smiled and gestured to the dining room. "Lunch is ready, isn't it, Mom?"

"Yes, it is. Come along, Teresa, and we'll discuss some ideas over lunch." Evelyn led the way into the dining room.

Evelyn took the seat at the head of the table and indicated Teresa should sit on her right, Jim on her left. After they were all seated, she picked up a small bell and rang it.

To Teresa's surprise, the door to the kitchen opened and a lady in a black maid's dress with a white apron entered the room with three plates. She skillfully delivered each one. Then she returned to the kitchen and got a tray with three glasses of iced tea.

"This looks delicious, Evelyn," Teresa said. At least, with the maid doing the work, she wouldn't be left alone with Jim.

"Yes, Maria is very good at her job."

Teresa didn't know what to say to that remark, so she concentrated on her lunch.

"How are you feeling, Teresa?" Jim asked.

Evelyn looked up sharply. "Is there something wrong, dear?"

"No, Evelyn. But I just found out I'm having twins."

"Oh, that's wonderful! What sexes?"

Teresa smiled at the woman's reaction. "Boys," she said softly.

"Have you chosen names for them?" Evelyn eagerly asked.

"I'm thinking about it. I'd like to name one of them after my father, Thomas. But I haven't decided on the other name. How did you choose your boys' names?"

"I named them after their father, Peter James Schofield."

"That was a nice thing to do." Before Teresa could get the forkful of chicken salad to her mouth, Jim spoke up.

"Don't you think the father should have some say in the names of his children?"

She put the fork down. "No. I don't think so. He's not going to have an active role in the babies' lives."

"How do you know?" he asked, sounding angry.

"Really, Jim, it isn't any of your business, is it?" Evelyn pointed out.

"I think it might be, Mom," Jim said mildly, but his eyes were hard as they stared at Teresa.

"Don't you dare," Teresa muttered.

"Why not? It's the truth."

"I didn't say it was!" Teresa stared back, determined to stop him.

"Children, what's going on here?" Evelyn stared at first one and then the other.

"Tell her!" Jim demanded.

"No, I won't."

Finally Jim tore his gaze from Teresa and turned to his mother. "Mom, I'm having tw—"

As if zapped by a cattle prod, Teresa jumped. "Evelyn, I have several nice colors for your living room. Perhaps we should look at them now."

Before his mother could respond, Jim reined in her attention. "As I was saying, Mom, I'm having tw—"

Teresa stood abruptly, nearly knocking over her chair as she pushed it back on the slick wood floor. "I'm afraid I have to go, Evelyn."

"But you haven't finished your lunch."

Teresa deliberately softened her voice. "I'm sorry. I—I'm not feeling well."

"Is it the babies?"

"No, the babies are fine." She bent down and kissed Evelyn's cheek. Then she headed for the front door.

Jim caught up to her before she reached it. "Teresa, you're being difficult."

"*I'm* being difficult? I don't think so." She wrenched her arm from his hold. "In case you don't know, usually the woman gets to announce the father of her babies. You have nothing to do with it!" Then she stormed out of the house.

Jim stood there, watching her go. Finally he returned to the dining table.

"Too bad about Teresa. I'll have to call her later." His mother took a sip of iced tea. "But you started to tell me something, Jim. What is it?"

He took a deep breath and blurted it out. "I'm the father of Teresa's babies."

"Don't be silly, dear. She would've told us if— What did you say?" Her cheeks paled and she stared at her son.

"I said I'm the father of Teresa's babies."

"But—but— When is the wedding?"

"I don't know. She doesn't seem to be interested." Jim picked up his fork and picked at the salad his mother had served.

"Have you asked her?" Evelyn asked. "I can't believe she'd turn you down. Especially if it's true that you and she—I mean, that you're the father."

"It's true."

"Well, then, I suggest you ask her to marry you at once. I won't have my grandchildren called bastards!"

"Mom, I can't—"

"Of course you can. She's a lovely young woman. And she's Tommie's sister. That's even better."

"I'm not sure we'll be happy, Mom."

"It's not about your happiness, son," Evelyn said, starch in her voice. "Obviously you've already had your fun, or she wouldn't be pregnant. But now you must assume your responsibilities. You can't continue to go about like a bachelor on the town when she's sitting home with your babies."

"I understand, Mother." He got up from his chair. "If you'll excuse me, I need to talk to Teresa."

He exited the house and got in his car. He intended to follow Teresa home, but he stopped at a fast-food drive-through and picked up some hamburgers.

Half an hour later, he parked in front of Teresa's house. When he got out, he grabbed the paper bag and two drinks, and closed the door with his foot. Then he crossed the small yard to Teresa's front door.

He managed to press the doorbell without spilling anything. Hearing her footsteps, he waited for the door to open.

It didn't.

"Go away," she said through the closed door.

"I've brought us some hamburgers."

"I'm not hungry!"

"You may not be, but your babies are. Open the door!"

Finally she did. "My babies are doing just fine. I don't need you to feed me."

Jim ignored her words and moved past her into the kitchen.

He had the burgers out of the bag by the time she joined him. "Do you have any ketchup?"

"Yes, but—"

"Mom's very upset that you didn't finish your lunch. In fact, you hardly ate anything."

"And whose fault is that?" Teresa pointed out.

"I know. I didn't intend to ruin your meal. That's why I brought over some food. Come on, sit down and eat. Please?"

"I *am* hungry…"

He pulled out her chair for her before she changed her mind. "

When she finished her burger, he said, "I'm glad you decided to eat. Now I have a question for you. Will you marry me?"

Chapter Five

His words surprised Teresa, but she hid any emotion. "No, thank you," she said simply, as if he'd offered her a drink.

"Why not?" he practically barked at her.

"Because I don't want to." He continued to stare at her and she smiled. "What's the matter, Jim? Did your attempt to embarrass me in front of your mother backfire on you?"

"What are you talking about?"

"Your mother insisted you ask me to marry you, didn't she?"

"Yeah, but I intended to ask you anyway."

"Ah, yes, such an emotional thing. You sounded like you were offering me some French fries. Just the way I'd always dreamed of being proposed to."

"I might have done a better job of asking you if you hadn't fallen asleep the other night when we were watching baseball!"

"Oh, I should've known it was all my fault." She stood and gathered the papers from their impromptu lunch and threw them away. Then she took a sponge and wiped off the table.

Jim sat there watching her, saying nothing.

When she finished tidying up, she left the kitchen.

Jim jumped to his feet and followed her until she went into her bedroom and closed the door. Frustrated, he banged on the door. "Teresa, we need to talk!"

She opened the door. "What about?"

"You know what about. I want to be a part of my sons' lives. I intend to be their father."

"So, when they get old enough to get around on their own, I'll let you have a reasonable amount of visitation." She started to close her bedroom door again, but he stuck his shoe in its path.

"That's not enough."

"It's all you get. Now get out of my house before I call the police."

He did as she requested, cursing under his breath.

Their private lunch hadn't gone well. What did she expect? Moonlight and roses? They were having babies. He'd done the honorable thing. And she'd thrown it back in his face.

Still debating what to do, he answered his cell phone. "Hello?"

"Jim, it's Tommie. They accepted your offer.

I've got the closing set for two weeks from today. Congratulations!"

"Thanks," he grumbled.

"What's wrong?" Tommie asked.

"I just asked your sister to marry me. She treated it like a joke."

"Did you tell her you were serious?"

"She knew. And she still refused. Can you talk to her?"

Tommie sighed. "I'll certainly talk to her, but I'm not promising anything."

"Okay, thanks. And the arrangements sound fine."

"Good. I'll talk to you later."

He shut off the phone, but he didn't have much hope that Tommie would convince Teresa to take his offer. Unreasonable woman!

Difficult man!

Teresa opened her bedroom door when she heard Jim close the door behind him. She went into the living room and watched him drive away.

She could take care of herself and her babies. That was no reason to marry him. People didn't penalize a woman for being a single parent these days. At least not much. And she'd told him he could have visitation.

What more did he want?

She went back to her workroom and went to work on her children's book.

She'd been writing for several hours when her phone rang. "Hello?"

"Did I interrupt you?" Tommie asked.

"What time is it?"

"It's almost four. Listen, I'm making meat loaf this evening and we thought it would be nice if you joined us."

"Oh, that's very nice of you, Tommie, but I think I'd better stay home tonight. I'm kind of tired. Maybe another night."

"You're sure everything is all right?"

"Yes, Mother Hen, I'm fine. Thanks for the invitation."

"You're welcome."

Teresa went back to her computer. She appreciated Tommie's invitation, but there was too much risk involved in dinner at her house. The risk of Jim being there.

Cheesecake in hand, Jim followed his brother into his kitchen. Tommie's meat loaf smelled great and the table was set like a magazine cover. But there were only three places.

"Only three for dinner tonight?" He tried for a light tone but failed.

"Who else did you expect?" Pete looked surprised.

Jim looked at Tommie. "I take it she refused?"

With a sigh, Tommie nodded. "But not because of you. She said she was too tired."

"But did you talk to her?" Jim persisted.

"No. I thought it would be better to talk to her in person."

"What are we talking about here?" Pete asked.

"I asked Teresa to marry me today and she refused."

"You did? What exactly did she say?"

"She said, 'No, thank you.'"

Before Pete could comment, Tommie carried the meat loaf to the table and told them to be seated. Pete asked the blessing and then began to pass the dishes to his brother.

"You'll convince her, Jim. Just don't let Mom know that you're the daddy until Teresa agrees," Pete warned with a grin.

Jim kept his head down. "Too late."

Pete stared at his brother. "You told Mom? Why?"

"I thought she might help me convince Teresa."

"Oh, no," Tommie said.

"What?" Jim asked, looking her way.

"Trying to pressure Teresa is the worst thing you can do. She was always the most stubborn of the three of us."

"More stubborn than you?" Pete asked. When she nodded, Pete looked sorrowfully at his brother. "Dude, you are in trouble."

"I just want what's best for my boys," Jim said, his voice pleading for agreement.

"What about Teresa?" Pete asked.

"What about her?"

"Oh, mercy, Jim, there's no way you'll convince Teresa to marry you with that attitude."

"I don't understand."

Pete tried to explain. "Marriage is about a lot more than kids, Jim. You have to live with the other person, share life and all the little things. And kids are happy if their parents are happy."

"I don't have anything against Teresa. She's beautiful, and the sweetest woman I know, but I'm not going to lie to her. I'm asking her to marry me because she's having my children."

"I think you have to get to know Teresa better," Tommie said. "Court her, why don't you? You were obviously doing well last summer or she wouldn't be pregnant now."

Jim didn't look thrilled with Tommie's suggestions. Finally, he muttered, "Don't you think we could negotiate? Wouldn't that be more honest? She wants the best for the boys as much as I do."

Tommie looked at Pete then she shrugged her shoulders. "You can try, but I doubt it will work."

She got up to clear the table. Jim helped take dishes to the sink. Then Tommie asked him to pour the coffee to accompany the dessert.

When they once again sat down at the table, enjoying the cheesecake, Jim looked at Tommie. "You'll still talk to her?"

"Of course, Jim. Did you tell her about the house you're buying?"

"The contract got approved?" Pete asked in surprise.

"Oh, yes, honey, I'm sorry I forgot to tell you. He'll close in two weeks."

"That's great, Jim. I can't wait to see it. Tommie told me it's wonderful."

"Yeah, Pete, it's really nice. And I guess I might as well sell my condo, since Teresa is being so stubborn. Can you list it for me?" Jim asked Tommie.

"Of course, if you're sure."

"I'm sure. I don't want the house sitting empty."

"Well, I think you should tell Teresa first. I don't think it will make a difference, but you never know."

"Okay, I'll call her tomorrow."

Why did he feel a sudden sense of dread?

Teresa slept late the next morning, only awakening when the doorbell rang about ten o'clock. She grabbed her robe and shrugged into it on the way to the front door. Through her peephole, she saw the delivery truck beside the curb and a man holding a bouquet of flowers at her door.

"Good morning," she said as she swung open the door, glad she'd braided her hair the night before.

"Good morning, ma'am. Teresa Tyler?"

"Yes, that's me." She stared at the beautiful bouquet, already in a glass vase. "Those are for me?" She loved flowers. They cheered up a room more than anything.

"Yes, ma'am. Just sign here."

After she'd signed, she carried the vase of beautiful flowers into her living room, setting the vase down on the coffee table. The bright flowers made her smile.

She reached for the discreet white card tucked among the blossoms. She was sure the flowers had come from her sisters. They were so thoughtful.

Much to her surprise, the card was signed by Jim. With only a few words. Gentle words. "I'm sorry."

What was he apologizing for? His behavior yesterday? Or because she was pregnant? She rubbed her tummy. She hoped he wasn't apologizing for their boys.

Already her children were such a part of her life, a part she wouldn't change even if she could. He didn't need to apologize for impregnating her. But his behavior yesterday… Yes, she'd accept his apology for that disgusting proposal of marriage, as if it were no more important than the burgers he'd bought for their lunch.

All day she received joy from the beautiful flowers. And she waited for the phone to ring. But Jim didn't call. To her surprise, neither did Evelyn. It was as if she'd had no impact on their lives.

She remembered reading somewhere that the ultimate insult was to be ignored.

With a sigh, Teresa reminded herself that yesterday she'd wanted him to go away, not to bother her. Now she had her wish.

And she hated it.

That evening she curled up in her bed and turned on her little television, the one she'd had in college. She pulled the covers over her to ward off a cold front coming through, and listened as the strong wind outside lowering the temperature even more. The babies were moving again, she realized as she clutched her stomach. It was as if they felt her uneasiness. She rubbed her stomach and softly sang a song her mother had used to soothe her and her sisters as small children.

To her surprise, the song did the trick. The babies

settled down. So did she. She fell asleep with the television on.

It was still playing when the doorbell awakened her the next morning. Again she grabbed her robe and hurried to the front door. Again she had a flower delivery.

After signing for the flowers, this time a more stylized arrangement, she took it to her bedroom and withdrew the card. Sinking onto the bed, she opened the small envelope.

Can we talk?

The question was followed by Jim's scrawled signature.

In exasperation, she stared at the flowers.

"We can't talk until you call, idiot!" she exclaimed. She almost ripped the card into pieces because of her frustration. The she smoothed the crumpled edges and carefully put it in her top dresser drawer, where it rested on top of the other card.

She took her shower, washing her long hair. Then she dried off and dressed. After combing the tangles out of her hair, she braided it. The braid was an old-fashioned style, but it suited her. She'd worn her hair like that ever since she was fourteen.

When the telephone rang, Teresa tensed. Then she chided herself. She'd wanted him to contact her, so what was she afraid of?

But the caller was Tommie, inviting her to dinner.

"Tommie, you don't have to worry. I'm eating well."

"That's not it. I promised Jim I would invite you.

He thinks you're more likely to talk to him if we're there. He wants to discuss your situation logically."

"He wants a group discussion?" Teresa asked in astonishment.

"Yes, I guess so."

Teresa closed her eyes, rocking back and forth as she sat on the bed.

"Teresa?"

"Yes, Tommie, I'll come to dinner. What shall I bring?"

Tommie chuckled. "I was hoping you'd ask that question. Can you make your carrot cake? You know how much I love it."

"Sure."

"Great! Jim will pick you up at—"

"No!" Teresa swallowed and calmed her voice. "I'll drive myself. What time shall I come?"

"But, Teresa—"

"I love you, Tommie, and I'm happy to accept your invitation. But I will drive myself."

"Okay, honey, but be careful."

"Of course." She hung up the phone, wondering how she'd ever survive the care her sisters insisted was necessary for her. She shrugged her shoulders. Maybe by the time she was nine months pregnant with twins and looked like a whale on stilts, she'd welcome it.

Jim paced the den, waiting for Teresa to arrive.

"I should've picked her up. Anything could happen to her. What if she had a flat?"

"Jim, calm down," Pete said from the leather sofa. "Teresa has a cell phone. She'd call if she was in trouble."

"Yeah, if she was conscious!" Jim returned, his fists clenched.

"You're supposed to be here to calmly discuss the future, Jim. Have you figured out what to say?"

Tommie leaned over the kitchen counter. "Pete? Your pasta is done."

"Damn. If she doesn't get here soon, it will be cold." Pete had become quite a cook, though his meals were simple. "Shall we go ahead and put the bread in the oven?"

Jim followed him into the kitchen as the doorbell rang.

He immediately reversed his direction toward the door. "No, brother," Pete said. "Let Tommie show her in. You need to make sure you know what you're going to say."

"I'm going to explain the benefits of us marrying for our children. It's the logical thing to do," Jim immediately said.

"That's no good," Pete told him.

"What do you mean?"

"You're not thinking straight, Jim. She obviously has some feelings for you or she wouldn't be pregnant. After all, she's Tommie's sister. How did that happen, anyway?"

"I don't know. I wasn't trying to make her feel anything. That's why I told her we couldn't... You know, be a couple."

"So you feel nothing for her?" Pete asked carefully.

Jim stared at the floor for a minute before he faced his brother, opening his mouth to speak. But Tommie's announcement cut him off.

"Teresa's here," she said as the women entered the kitchen. "And she brought her carrot cake for dessert."

Pete closed the oven door and stepped over to kiss Teresa's cheek. "Welcome, Teresa."

"Thank you, Pete. Jim."

As a greeting, it lacked a lot of warmth, but Jim figured maybe he deserved it. He nodded his head. "You look lovely tonight."

"Thank you. Dinner smells good, Pete."

"It's my famous spaghetti," Pete said with a grin. "My repertoire is kind of small."

"I'm sure Tommie appreciates the effort," Teresa said, smiling first at Pete and then Tommie.

Jim noticed that her smile didn't extend to him.

"Time to eat," Pete announced.

"Take a seat," Tommie ordered as she carried glasses of iced tea to the table. When they still didn't move, Tommie added, "You two sit on that side of the table. Pete and I will sit over here."

Jim pulled out a chair for Teresa, then took the one beside her.

As he looked up at Tommie and Pete, their gazes were zeroed in on him. Loaded and ready. All he needed was a cigarette and a last wish. He was already facing the firing squad.

Chapter Six

Much to Teresa's surprise, dinner was enjoyable. By the end of the meal, she'd relaxed, laughing at Pete and Tommie's silly sparring. Even Jim, sitting beside her, had laughed at their antics. He'd also contributed to the conversation and actually smiled at Teresa twice.

She'd counted.

She got another look when he took his first bite of the cake she'd made.

"You made this? And it really has carrots in it?" he asked, looking at her.

"Haven't you had carrot cake before?" she asked.

"No. I've seen cakes in bakeries with a little orange carrot on the icing, but it never appealed to me. This is good," he added with a smile.

"Thank you." She actually smiled at him.

After they'd finished their dessert and moved to the den, Teresa felt herself tensing up again. She didn't want to discuss her babies logically…or her heart.

They'd barely sat down when Jim blurted out, "I have something to tell you, Teresa."

She remained silent, just looking at him.

He cleared his throat. "Do you remember that house you and Tommie looked at, the one with the perfect backyard?"

"Oh, yes. It was wonderful," Teresa said, smiling at the memory.

Softly, quietly, Jim said, "I bought it."

She looked at him with wonder in her eyes. Hope.

"I want my boys to have a good home, to play in that backyard," he added.

So that was the reason. For his boys. They were what counted, not her. She bowed her head, hiding the hope that was dying in her eyes.

"I want you to move in there now. I'll stay in the condo, so…there won't be any awkwardness, until you agree to marry me."

"No, Jim. *You* should go ahead and move in. Then, when the boys are old enough to visit, you'll already be there. It was very thoughtful of you to think of their happiness when they are older." She stood, without looking at anyone. "Thank you for a lovely evening. I need to go now. Pregnant women go to bed early, you know." She left the room, with Tommie following.

"Are you all right, honey?" Tommie asked.

"Of course, Tommie, I'm fine, just tired." But she refused to look her sister in the eye.

"Jim was hoping the house would encourage you."

"It did. He obviously wants to provide for his children. That's very nice."

"But—"

"I have to go," Teresa said and pulled open the door. Then she ran down the sidewalk, wanting to make sure she was alone when she burst into tears.

Jim was pacing the floor again when Tommie returned to the den. He railed on her immediately. "It didn't work. She doesn't want to live there. I thought you said she loved it."

"She did. And she still does. Oh, Jim, didn't you see? When you first told her about the house, she was delighted. Then you removed that joy."

"How? How did I do that?"

Pete sighed. "You told her you bought the house for the boys."

"Well, I did! What's wrong with that?"

"What about Teresa?"

"I said she should move in now." Jim looked at his brother and sister-in-law in confusion.

"Jim," Tommie said softly, "what Pete means is you didn't include Teresa in the future. You didn't include Teresa in buying that house."

"Yes, I did. I had you show it to Teresa before I bought it."

"But you didn't tell her that. All you talked about was buying it for the children. The picture you showed Teresa was one of you and your children in a beautiful place, but she didn't feel a part of it." Tommie slowly shook her head. "I think she was on the verge of tears when she left."

"Damn it! Why didn't she say something?" Jim demanded.

Pete took his brother by the arm. "Come on, Jim. There's something I want to show you in my study."

Jim said nothing on the walk to the other side of the house. Once they reached the study, Pete closed the door and told his brother to have a seat.

"What do you want to show me?" Jim asked.

"I don't have anything to show you. I want to ask you the question I asked you earlier. How do you feel about Teresa?"

Jim closed up. Pete could see it, and he wanted to shake his brother and make him open up. But they'd never really talked since that debacle during their senior year. While Jim had dated since then, he'd been very careful not to become emotionally involved.

"She's sweet. A good person."

"Tommie wants you to love her sister. Not just the babies she's carrying."

Jim jumped up from his chair and began pacing again. "I respect her," he said stubbornly.

"When are you going to forget what happened our last year of high school, Jim?"

"That has nothing to do with what's happening today." Jim paced again. "How do I get her to move into the house?"

"I don't know. I suspect she won't. Like Tommie, she's very independent."

"A lot of help you are," Jim said in disgust. "I'm going home."

Morning dawned but Teresa stayed in bed. She'd spent a restless night, feeling the babies move, crooning to them. That was how she'd fallen asleep. Now she lay there, rubbing her belly, thinking about what the boys would be like. What would they look like? Would they have Jim's dark hair and green eyes, or her fair features?

Her reverie was cut short by the doorbell. Shrugging in her robe, she rushed to the door, sure she was receiving more flowers.

Instead, she found Jim on her doorstep.

She blinked several times before she spoke. "Jim, what are you doing here?"

"I need to talk to you. Did I— Did I wake you up?"

"Uh, no," Teresa said, tugging the tie on her robe tighter.

"I brought some doughnuts," he said, making his way to the kitchen.

"Oh, uh, thank you. I'll go get dressed." She escaped to her bedroom. Catching a glimpse of herself in the mirror, she sank to the bed in horror. Then, realizing she had little time, she hurriedly dressed and rebraided her hair. With a light touch, she added a little makeup. Finally ready to face the world, or Jim, she hurried back to her kitchen.

Jim jumped to his feet and gestured for her to sit opposite him where a cup of coffee waited.

"Oh, I can't drink coffee. I'll have to have orange juice."

"No coffee? I thought you liked coffee?"

"I do, but the doctor doesn't want me to have the caffeine." While she was talking, she poured the coffee into the sink and got down a glass, filling it with orange juice.

"Should I switch to orange juice, too?" he asked, concerned.

"No, you can have your coffee. I got over the morning sickness a few weeks ago." She couldn't hold back a shudder at the memory of mornings spent throwing up.

"Was it hard?"

Teresa shrugged her shoulders. "It wasn't fun."

"Have the babies been moving again?"

"Yes. It's coming more frequently now."

He stared at her stomach.

Feeling awkward, she reached for a doughnut. "May I?"

"Yeah, sure, I brought them for you…and me, too, of course. I wasn't sure whether you would've already had breakfast, but I hoped you'd like them anyway."

"Yes, I have a sweet tooth," she said with a rueful grin.

"When do you go back to the doctor?"

Teresa had come to terms with her hopes and dreams last night. She wasn't going to have the relationship she'd wished for with Jim. But these were his babies as well as hers. As much as she hadn't wanted to admit that fact to her family, it was too late now. She should share whatever he wanted to know about the children. "I only go once a month until I get closer to term, so it will be several weeks away."

"May I go with you?"

"If you want, as long as you don't come in the room for the examination." She had the right to some modesty.

Jim appeared shocked by her agreement. "Thank you."

"You're welcome. After all, we both know these are your babies as well as mine."

Jim released a pent-up breath. "That's really wonderful of you, Teresa."

She smiled but said nothing.

"So you'll move into the house when I've closed on it?"

Her head snapped up and she stared at him. "What makes you think that?"

"You said you understood that these are my babies. I assumed that meant you would let me take care of you."

Teresa took a sip of orange juice to stall. Then, calmly, she said, "Jim, I don't need anyone to take care of me. I'm fine here. There's no need for me to move temporarily to your house."

"Temporarily? I thought we were going to marry." He gave her a hard stare.

"No. I can't marry you, Jim. I know how much you fear you'll be trapped. For the sake of my children, I can't marry you."

"What do you mean, for the sake of the babies?

That's the very reason we need to marry. So they aren't bastards!" Jim was practically leaping from his chair.

Teresa took a deep breath. The acid of the orange juice, combined with the emotion in their discussion, wasn't making her tummy feel good. "I think it's better for them to be bastards than for them to know their father hates their mother."

This time Jim stood up. He put his hands on the table and leaned over. "I don't hate you!"

"You will if you marry me, Jim, and we both know it. I hope someday you'll find someone who will be important enough to you to break that barrier, but it's not me."

Jim raised his voice until he was shouting. "That's not true!"

Teresa's stomach ended the conversation. She ran to the kitchen sink and lost what little breakfast she'd had.

"Are you all right?" Jim asked, hovering over her.

Slowly, Teresa straightened, turning on the water to rinse off her face and clean the sink. "Just go, Jim. If you have questions about the babies, you can call me. Otherwise, leave me alone."

Jim glared at her. Then he turned and left the house.

Teresa went to bed. She needed calm, security. Curled up in her bed, she dozed off.

Tommie's call woke her half an hour later. "Teresa, are you all right?"

"I'm fine," she said calmly.

"Jim said he upset you."

"So what else is new?" she asked, knowing her sister wouldn't believe her if she lied.

"He didn't tell me why you were upset, but he was worried."

"I'm sure he was. He's worried about his children."

"I'm sure—"

"I'm not," Teresa interrupted. "It's all right, sis. I've come to terms with the situation. I've told him I'll let him know the babies. I'm not trying to shut him out."

"What about marrying him?"

"That would be a big mistake. He has this phobia about being forced into marriage, about being trapped. I'm not going to marry him."

Again, Teresa could feel her stomach churning. She hurriedly got off the phone with her sister and lay back down, deep-breathing the entire time.

She fell back asleep and didn't awaken until the phone rang a little after two o'clock.

"Teresa? It's Evelyn. How are you, dear?"

"I'm fine, Evelyn. How are you?"

"I'm wonderful! I've been out shopping for baby items. I'm so excited about our babies."

Teresa groaned silently. "That's very nice, Evelyn. But, you know, it's a few months before they're born."

"I know, dear, but I'm having so much fun. Of course, I also have to find a wedding present that will look good in your new home!"

Teresa closed her eyes. Then she said, "Evelyn, Jim's new house is lovely. But I'm not going to move there, and we're not going to be married."

"That's ridiculous. You have to marry for the sake of your children!"

"Talk to Jim, Evelyn, please. I can't— This is too difficult. I have to go."

She hung up the phone, feeling ashamed of her behavior, but she'd had enough emotional confrontations for today. She got up and stumbled to the kitchen to make herself some lunch. She needed to get stronger. Then she would work on her book. Thinking about the readers, young children with their inquisitiveness and fanciful take on life, calmed her.

For the next three weeks, Teresa avoided contact with her sisters and Jim. Unfortunately, she had to deal with some phone calls, but she remained adamant that she had to stay at home. Any invitation from Tommie always had the possibility of including Jim, and Teresa definitely wasn't up for that.

She did talk to her mother every week, but her mother didn't try to persuade her to do anything. She was a good listener. They also discussed her and Joel's wedding plans.

By the end of the third week, Teresa was getting a little lonely. She called her neighbor, Mrs. Patterson, and invited her to dinner.

Though there was fifty years difference in their ages, Teresa and her plump, white-haired neighbor had forged a friendship from the day Teresa moved in. Mrs. Patterson was the only friend Teresa had in the neighborhood. She'd become a surrogate grandma, or a favorite aunt, dispensing wise advice when called upon and all the time offering a cheery smile to lift her spirits.

"Hello, my dear. How's the little mother-to-be?" Mrs. Patterson asked as she entered the house.

"Feeling fat and lonely."

"I think you look quite trim, considering you're what, five months?"

"Almost."

"And how could you possibly be lonely with your sisters around?"

Teresa waved for her friend to follow her to the breakfast room. "I've refused to see them."

Mrs. Patterson sat down at the table, watching Teresa as she began putting food on the table. But she didn't respond until Teresa had joined her at the table. "Why would you avoid your sisters?"

Teresa sighed. "You're going to think I'm crazy."

"No, dear, that's impossible."

Teresa smiled. "That must be why I called you and not them. They both think I'm crazy."

"Why?"

"Because I've refused to marry the father of my babies."

Again her friend asked, "Why?"

"Because he doesn't love me. Even more than that, he's had a fear of being trapped into marriage. Which is exactly what I would be doing if I married him."

"Then I think you made the right decision."

"Do you really? That makes me feel so much better."

"I'm glad, my dear. I'm a little surprised that your

sisters would urge you to marry him. Do they know about his fear?"

"Yes, he's Tommie's brother-in-law. And he's bought a beautiful four-bedroom house for the babies."

"Babies? Are you having a multiple birth?"

"Oh, I forgot I hadn't told you that. Yes, I'm having twin boys. That's why my sisters want me to marry Jim. They're afraid I won't be able to make it on my own."

"It won't be easy, my dear, but of course you'll be able to make it on your own. After all, I'll be next door. And I love little boys. I have three of them, you know."

Except that her "little boys" were strapping men, all grown up and over six feet tall. "I know. I'll need a lot of information, because I only know about little girls."

"There are quite a few differences, I think. But I'm sure you can handle them. After all, you have a lot of little boys in your classes."

"That's true."

"If the father pays child support, I'm sure you'll be all right."

"I haven't asked him to pay anything."

"Don't be so proud, Teresa. They are his babies, too."

"I know. I'd hoped to keep his identity secret until after their birth. Now he wants to go to the doctor visits with me."

"Of course he does. And I believe your sisters are thinking your life will be easier if you go ahead and marry him."

"But that's not true. I would be miserable married to him, because I—" she stopped before the admission slipped out. But what the heck? This was Mrs. Patterson, after all. She looked the woman straight in the eye and said what she'd told no one else. "I love him. I loved him the night the babies were conceived, and I haven't stopped loving him…but to live with him, knowing he didn't love me, would be terrible."

"Yes, it would. I don't think I could do that, even if it would be good for the children."

The pair ate in silence for a moment. Finally, Teresa said, "Do you think it *would* be good for the boys?"

"I always think the child gets the best start in life with both parents around. It doesn't mean you can't do a good job of raising them on your own. After all, your mother did."

"And I'll have you to give me advice," Teresa said, trying to smile as if she didn't have a care in the world.

"Of course. And I'll tell my children I can't possibly move. You need me too much!" Mrs. Patterson exclaimed.

"Are they trying to get you to move?" Teresa asked.

"Yes, my dear. They tell me I'm too old to live alone. But that's not true. I have everything as I want it in my little house. I love it there."

"I know. I feel the same way about my place. Of course, I'll have to make changes to accommodate the boys."

"I assume you're going to give up your workroom for them. Will you continue to write?"

"Yes. I've actually finished the first draft. I've gone through it twice and I'm very happy with it."

"That's wonderful!" Mrs. Patterson exclaimed. "You have so much talent, Teresa."

"I'm not sure about that, but I find the writing to be very satisfying. I lose myself in it and don't think about my situation."

"That's good. I think you need to stay calm when you're pregnant."

"I've proved that. The last conversation I had with Jim, he began yelling at me and I lost my breakfast." She leaned in conspiratorially and added, "At least it stopped him from yelling at me anymore."

"You need to tell him he should avoid yelling at you."

"Maybe if he yells at me again, I'll send him to you to explain that to him," Teresa said with a laugh.

"I like to hear you laugh, child."

"I've missed laughing." She took a sip of her iced tea. "Oh, did I tell you my mother is getting married?"

She shook her head. "That's wonderful, isn't it?"

"Absolutely. Joel is a wonderful man and he loves Mom. She spent so many years on her own, raising us. I'm glad she can finally live for herself and Joel. They are so sweet together."

"Which makes your own situation more difficult?" Mrs. Patterson asked softly.

The woman was so wise, so intuitive, she identified Teresa's emotions even though she herself hadn't. She wasn't jealous of her mother; she could never be. Ann Tyler deserved every ounce of her long-overdue happiness. It was just that her mother's wedding made her even more conscious of the lack of her own.

"In some ways it does," she admitted, "but I'm still very happy for them."

"I know you are, dear." Mrs. Patterson smiled at her. "Now how about some of that wonderful dessert I smell?"

"I made your favorite, peach cobbler," Teresa said as she got up to get it. "With ice cream to go on top."

"I can't believe you remembered."

"Well, it just so happens it's my favorite, too," Teresa confessed. As she passed, she bent down to hug the elderly woman, not only for her insights and comfort, but for knowing when to put an end to them.

They enjoyed their dessert, discussing a pair of blankets Mrs. Patterson promised to make. She even gave Teresa a few pointers.

"One thing to remember, Teresa, even if you're going to use disposable diapers—and I don't blame you if you do—you'll still need some cloth diapers. They make wonderful burping cloths."

"They do? I hadn't thought of that."

"Yes, and in the beginning, your babies will need at least three outfits a day. They'll spit up on everything. Even if you wipe them up, the smell is unpleasant."

"Good heavens, the laundry must really pile up."

"You'll feel like it's multiplying in the dark," Mrs. Patterson said with a smile.

"Oh, my. How will I keep up?"

"The best way is to hire some help. Because you

won't get much sleep unless you go to bed every time the babies do."

"But I can't do that. I'll never get everything done."

"Now you see why your sisters are worried about you being on your own?"

"I suppose," Teresa said. Then she changed the subject. "More dessert?"

"Gracious no, my dear. I guess it's time I head home, too. You know I like to go to bed at ten."

"I know. But I can't thank you enough for coming. I feel so much better about everything," Teresa told her friend with a smile.

"I'm glad, my dear."

Teresa walked her to the door, offering to walk her home.

"Don't be silly, child. I'm just next door. Stay inside where you belong."

Teresa closed the door behind her, thinking about how much Mrs. Patterson meant to her. She had been the one to suggest Teresa start writing a children's book. And she'd never condemned her for getting pregnant out of wedlock.

She walked down the hall toward her bedroom, thinking of going to bed, too. She was pleasantly tired, but she was at peace about her life. That was the effect Mrs. Patterson had on her. Teresa hoped she had that much wisdom and patience when she was that old.

With a sigh, she entered her bedroom, looking forward to a good night's sleep.

Just as she started to remove her knit top, she

heard a bloodcurdling scream. Immediately she feared it was Mrs. Patterson. She didn't hesitate. Grabbing a baseball bat she kept near her bed, she raced for the front door.

Chapter Seven

From the sound of the weeping Teresa knew it was Mrs. Patterson. She sprinted in the dark toward the house next door, until her foot turned on something hard and unseen and found herself falling. The babies were all she could think of and she curled her body into a ball to protect them as she hit the ground. She rolled several times until her head struck some rocks Mrs. Patterson had used to separate her flower bed from the rest of the yard.

"Teresa, is that you?"

Teresa tried to answer her neighbor's call, but found it difficult to get the words out. She tried to get up but quickly fell again when her ankle couldn't support her weight. She found her voice. "Mrs. Patterson?" she called, whether to comfort her friend or get help for herself she didn't know.

Suddenly Mrs. Patterson was beside her. "Teresa, I didn't mean to frighten you! Are you all right?"

"I fell. I think I hurt my ankle."

"Oh, dear, I'll try to help you up."

"I can use the bat as leverage. I heard you scream. What's wrong?"

"My house is ruined!"

"What? Did someone break in?"

"Yes! I think it must've been the Westside Burglar. He destroyed anything he didn't take. It's awful!"

"Have you called 9-1-1?" Teresa asked, grimacing at the pain in her ankle now that she was standing. And she must be sweating heavily as there was moisture on her forehead.

"I'll go call at once. But I can't leave you— Teresa, you're bleeding!"

"I am?"

"Yes, on your forehead. I'll get a cloth. Just a minute!"

As the woman ran into the house, Teresa insisted, "Call 9-1-1 first!"

As she sat there, Teresa raised a hand to her forehead and felt the sticky liquid and the cut she'd sustained. All around her, the night grew darker and the trees swayed, until she thought she'd topple once more. Then Mrs. Patterson returned.

"They're sending someone at once."

"Good."

"Now you lay your head in my lap so I can clean up the blood. How did you hurt your head?"

Teresa did as Mrs. Patterson asked, finding it easier not to hold her head up. "I fell and rolled to protect the babies. I hit my head on those rocks." She waved her hand in the direction of the flower bed.

"I'm so sorry! I think I should call for an ambulance. This cut looks deep and it keeps bleeding."

It was late when Jim finally left the accounting firm where he was a partner. He'd worked all day and night on a proposal for a big client. Though he was doing well financially, if he pulled off this deal, he'd be able to buy just about anything he wanted.

Except Teresa.

Somehow, he'd believed she'd come around, give in to the pressure of being a single mom and make a family with him. Without his having to do anything.

Jim realized he was a coward when it came to emotions. He didn't like facing that fact. But there it was. He didn't know if he loved Teresa or not. And he was afraid to find out.

"Damn!" he said, hitting the steering wheel. Tired of hearing himself think, he turned on the radio. He kept it on the all-news station because he frequently missed the early or late TV news. He picked up the latest report in progress.

"…struck again. This time the thief that police have dubbed the Westside Burglar hit a private home on Oak Street on the west side of town. Police have released no other details…."

Jim heard nothing else. His mind stopped processing after he heard the address—Oak Street. Teresa lived on Oak! He jammed on the brakes and fumbled for his cell phone, glad there was no traffic this time of night. When he got no answer at her house, his worst fears started to take shape. He tried Tommie's, but Teresa wasn't there either.

So that he didn't panic Tommie, he feigned calm and said, "I'm sure she's all right, maybe she's all right, maybe she's just sleeping through the phone. I'll go check on her."

"Let me know that everything's all right, Jim," Tommie made him promise.

Flipping the phone shut, he made a U-turn and sped down the street. It was only minutes, but it felt like hours, till he turned onto her street. He saw a police car flashing in the driveway right next to Teresa's house, and several people standing at the front porch. None of them was the woman he was looking for.

He ran to Teresa's front door and pounded on it, but he waited in vain for her answer.

"Sir?"

At the voice behind him, Jim turned around to see one of the police officers approaching.

"Yes?"

"Are you a friend of Miss Tyler?"

"Yes, why?"

"Well, she's been injured and—"

The policeman gestured toward the other house and Jim didn't wait for him to finish his sentence. He sprinted in that direction. "Teresa?"

Those standing at the porch parted to reveal Teresa sitting on the grass, blood streaking down the left side of her face.

Jim fell to his knees in front of her. "Honey, what happened?"

"I fell."

"You're bleeding." He turned to the people around her. "Can't you do something about that?"

An elderly woman spoke up. "We've sent for the ambulance, but—"

"I'll take her to the hospital." Jim stood and reached for her.

"Wait. Here's a cloth to wipe the wound with," the old lady said. "I'm so sorry this happened."

Jim thanked her and handed the cloth to Teresa. Then he swung her into his arms.

The police officer stopped him. "Sir, before you go, you should know that the burglar has the keys to her house. She shouldn't come back to the house to-night. And the locks should be changed."

"How did—" Jim began.

"The house next door was hit. The old lady kept Miss Tyler's spare key, carefully labeled on a hook in the kitchen. The guy saw his next opportunity." The officer's voice sobered. "This guy destroys as much as he steals. He's one angry pervert."

"Thanks, Officer."

He carried Teresa to his car. As he put her in, she demanded he make sure Mrs. Patterson had some-where to go.

Wanting to do whatever would comfort Teresa, he went back and checked on the older woman.

"Thank you for asking, but I've called my son. He's going to pick me up in a few minutes. And I don't think I'll ever come back here. I'd be too scared."

Jim pulled out a business card and wrote his home number on the back. "If you want to talk to Teresa, call this number. If she's not there, I'll know where to find her."

"Oh, thank you. I don't want to lose touch with Teresa. She's such a sweet girl. And it's my fault she's injured."

"Why?" Jim asked, puzzled.

"She heard me scream when I came into my house. She thought I was being attacked and she ran to help me."

The policeman said, "Here's her weapon." He held out a baseball bat. "She's one brave woman."

"Yes, she is," Jim agreed, giving a silent prayer of thanks that the burglar had already gone.

He again said goodbye and hurried to his car. Teresa looked as if she was asleep, but he was afraid that was caused by the head wound. "Teresa, wake up. You need to stay awake until we see the doctor. "You might have a concussion."

She blinked several times then she closed her eyes again.

After he pulled away from the curb, he reached out to shake her. "Teresa, stay awake. How are the babies?"

That woke her. "I think they're okay. When I twisted my ankle, I rolled several times into the rock."

"Wipe your face, honey. The blood's still coming down."

Seeing the hospital just ahead of him, he drove into the emergency parking lot. Wasting no time, he ran around the car and picked her up in his arms.

As they came through the double doors, a nurse immediately told an orderly to get them a wheelchair. Jim settled Teresa into it and pushed her to the desk.

The nurse asked the nature of her injuries.

"She has a head wound that continues to bleed, and she said she twisted her ankle," Jim said, glad to get her to someone who could help her. "And she's pregnant with twins, almost five months."

"And you are…"

Jim's cheeks flushed. "I'm a friend."

"And her husband is…?"

"She doesn't have a husband. Can't you get someone to do something about the bleeding?" he asked.

The nurse picked up a phone and spoke to someone. "We're going to look at her wounds. But you'll have to stay here."

"Fine!" Jim responded, anger in his voice. He took a step away from the desk as they wheeled Teresa into a curtained area and called Tommie again. He'd barely given her an update when she cut him off.

"We're on our way."

Jim paced the waiting area constantly until he saw Pete and Tommie enter. He hurried to them. "They won't tell me anything!"

"I'll ask if they'll let me see her," Tommie said, patting him on the arm.

When Tommie approached the desk, she told the nurse she was Teresa's sister and she wanted to see her. The woman directed her to the second curtain.

Tommie waved to the two men and disappeared behind the curtain.

Jim stood there, staring at the curtains, jealous as hell that Tommie could see her but he couldn't.

"How badly was she hurt?" Pete asked.

"She twisted her ankle and hit her head on a rock. She has a cut at the top of her forehead that I'm sure will require stitches. She fell asleep in the car and I was afraid it was a concussion. But they haven't told me anything since I'm not a family member!"

"Frustrating, isn't it?" Pete said.

"It's not anything that you've experienced!" Jim exclaimed.

"You're right. I'm married to Tommie. That gives me special status. If you're not married to Teresa before she gives birth to those babies, you're going to be standing on the outside, waiting for information."

Jim clenched his teeth, saying nothing. He'd asked her to marry him. It wasn't his fault.

Was it?

He didn't like that thought. He knew Teresa wanted more than he was offering. She wanted him to offer his heart. Damn it, he'd promised to take care of her and the babies. Tonight, he hadn't hesitated to go to her house to see if she was all right. He'd immediately made sure she was safe.

Taken her into his arms. Carried her to his car.

For a few moments he'd cared for her. Then they'd gotten to the hospital and he'd become a stranger.

Tommie appeared, immediately drawing Jim's attention. He hurried to her. "How is she? What have they done? Has she stopped bleeding?"

"Easy, Jim. Give her a chance to answer," Pete said.

Tommie sent her husband a grateful smile. Then she looked at Jim. "The bleeding stopped, but she needed five stitches. They had to shave a little hair, so don't mention it, if you can help it."

Jim drew a deep breath. "What about her ankle?"

"It's a severe sprain. The doctor doesn't want her on it for about a week. Then she has to come back to let him look at it again."

As she finished, Jim saw the curtain open and a wheelchair came out, pushed by a doctor.

Jim moved forward, his gaze scanning Teresa's face. She looked exhausted. "How are you, honey?"

"Fine."

"Who is taking her home?" the doctor asked.

"We will," Tommie said.

"No," Jim said. "Is she allowed to use crutches?"

"After a couple of days," the doctor said.

"Well, you have a two-story house. She can't go up and down the stairs. So she should stay with me."

Tommie began to protest. "Jim, I don't think—"

Jim leaned closer. "I'll take good care of her, Tommie."

"But I don't want her pressured," she said solemnly, staring at Jim.

"I won't, I promise."

"Now that we've got that settled," the doctor said in a sarcastic tone. "I need to give you some instructions."

Jim listened carefully.

"I don't think she has a concussion, but I'd like you to wake her up every three hours and ask her her name and another question or two to be sure she's all right. But I want her to sleep as much as she wants to. She was definitely shocked and she'll need several days to recover."

"Of course. And the babies?" Jim asked anxiously.

"They're fine. They've moved a lot since she came in. They are highly cushioned in her stomach."

Jim wasn't pleased with the man's attitude, but he took over the handles to the wheelchair. "All right, we'll be back in a week for you to examine her ankle."

The doctor put his hand on Jim's arm. "The orderly will push her to the door. You go get your car and meet them there."

Jim didn't want to turn loose of Teresa's chair, but he had no choice. "Fine." With a nod to his brother and Tommie, he went out the automatic doors.

When he pulled the car to the door, he got out and hurried to the passenger side. After opening the door, he lifted Teresa into his arms and put her in the front seat.

"Where are we going?" Teresa asked, her voice weak.

"Home," Jim said.

Pete leaned into the open car. "Tommie and I are going to pack a bag for Teresa. We'll be over to your house in about half an hour."

"Okay. See you then." He hoped they didn't take

long. He didn't think Teresa would be awake long. She seemed a little out of it right now.

After he'd negotiated the emergency parking lot, he pulled out onto the road that would lead to their neighborhood. He was anxious to get Teresa home, in his house. As he pulled into his lighted garage, he looked over at her.

She was asleep, her head resting on the window of her door. He killed the car engine and came around the car to gently open her door. "Teresa, we're home."

Her eyes fluttered open. "It doesn't look like home," she muttered.

"It's *my* home. Remember? With the wonderful backyard?"

"Yes, it was a wonderful place," she said dreamily.

"Yes, and you're going to stay here with me until you're well." And until they at least got new locks on her house. He'd prefer that she made her move permanent. He didn't like her living alone in that neighborhood. Somehow, he'd have to convince her to stay.

"Sit still. I'm going to carry you into the house. By the time you're ready to get around, you'll have a pair of crutches."

He lifted her into his arms after opening the door. It felt good to carry her, to know she was safe. He got them into the den and put her down on the sofa. "Your sister is bringing you clothes. Would you like something to eat or drink while you wait?"

"I'd like some water. I feel like I've been chewing cotton."

"Coming right up."

As he stepped around the couch to enter the connecting kitchen, Teresa sat up, her head showing over the couch. "It's very pretty."

"Thanks, but shouldn't you be lying down?"

"I don't think the doctor said I should go to bed right away. Are you sure I shouldn't go to my house? I don't want to be any trouble."

Jim waited until he handed her some water. "Honey, you can't stay there until you get the locks changed. The burglar got your extra keys from Mrs. Patterson's house."

Teresa frowned. "Why would Mrs. Patterson give them to him?"

The doorbell rang and Jim told her he'd be back in a minute.

He opened the door to his brother and Tommie. To his surprise, they carried a suitcase and a pizza box.

"What's this?"

Pete grinned. "I thought someone might be hungry, so I called in an order while Tommie was packing Teresa's clothes and we picked it up on the way."

"What kind is it?" Jim asked.

"Well, I thought that was interesting," Pete said as they walked to the den.

"What do you mean?" Jim asked, not sure what he was referring to.

"You and Teresa like the same kind—hamburger with extra cheese."

Jim looked at his brother, surprise on his face. Then he smiled. "Sounds good to me."

Teresa smiled at her sister. "Did you bring me some clothes? I kind of bled all over this shirt."

"Yes, but you'd better put on your nightgown and robe, because you'll be going to bed soon. Come on, I'll help you change."

"Wait, I'll carry her," Jim insisted.

"I could hop on one leg with Tommie's help," Teresa said.

"Not necessary," Jim assured her. He swooped her up and carried her down the hall to his bedroom. "She'll be sleeping in here."

"But where will you be sleeping?" Tommie asked. "You don't have any other bed."

"I'll be sleeping on the couch." He set Teresa down on the bed. "Let me know when she's ready."

Then he headed back to the den where Pete was waiting.

"Did you have any trouble finding Teresa's things?"

"Nope. The police were still there, but with Tommie along, I didn't have any trouble convincing them they were sisters. While Tommie was inside, they told me about the burglar getting her keys. What are you going to do about it?"

"I'm going to call a locksmith to meet me over there in the morning and get all the locks changed. I don't want her to move back there, but I don't want the place destroyed, either."

"Jim?" Tommie called from the bedroom.

"I'll go get our ladies. Then we can have some pizza. I never got any dinner."

When he carried Teresa into the den, she was wearing a blue robe that made her eyes look huge. "We're going to have some pizza as a late-night snack."

Pete had gotten out some plates and found some caffeine-free drinks in the pantry. Soon they were all eating pizza, but it wasn't too long before Jim noticed Teresa getting sleepier.

"Teresa, are you ready to go to bed?"

"Yes, I'm tired. Can you take me home?"

Pete and Tommie started to speak but Jim's voice halted them. "Sure, honey, I'll take you home." He picked her up and walked down the hall to his bedroom and slid her into the bed and tucked the covers around her. "I'll see you in the morning."

When he came back in the den, Tommie stared at him. "Are you sure she'll be all right? Does she know where she is?"

"She's fine, just a little confused. Or, stubborn, if I know her." He shook his head. "Don't worry. Yes. I'll check on her through the night, but she's already sound asleep. And I'll get Mom to come sit with her when I go to meet the locksmith in the morning."

"Then we'll be on our way," Pete said, taking Tommie's hand. "Come on, honey. You can trust Jim."

Once he'd closed the door behind them, Jim gathered up a pillow and blanket for the couch. But when he passed by his bedroom, he couldn't help but look at his guest, sleeping soundly in his bed. He was glad she was safe in his house.

He stared at Teresa, curled up on her side, cradling his children. He hadn't thought much about the babies this evening, other than to ask the doctor if they were okay.

He was concerned with Teresa.

That was an eye-opener for him. He'd told himself that he was only interested in his children. But tonight he'd discovered he was concerned about Teresa, too.

Maybe, he thought, he was even more concerned about her than the boys. Because they weren't here yet. They didn't seem real. But Teresa was real. And he wanted her in his life.

The urge to join her in that bed, to touch her and hold her, was so powerful, he hurried to the den, afraid he'd turn Pete's words to Tommie—*You can trust Jim*—into a lie.

Chapter Eight

Someone was trying to wake her up.

"What?" she muttered, trying to hide beneath the covers.

"What's your name?"

Teresa frowned. Why would someone be in her bedroom asking such a strange question? "Teresa Tyler, of course."

"Don't go back to sleep yet."

"Why not?" she asked crossly, keeping her eyes shut.

"Are you pregnant?"

"Yes. Can't you tell by looking?"

"What are you having?"

"Twin boys."

"Can I feel them move?"

"Sure, if I can go back to sleep," she agreed with a sigh.

She felt a warm hand splayed on her stomach. She guided it to a certain spot and moved it back and forth, hoping the boys would calm down.

Gradually, she returned to sleep.

Jim sat with his hand on Teresa's stomach, amazed that she could sleep while her babies moved as much as they did. Amazed that these movements were made by his children. Amazed that she was letting him touch her.

He lay down on the bed, on top of the covers, his hand still covering her stomach. He just wanted to understand how a husband would feel. How he would hold his future in his hands.

Would Teresa understand if she awoke? Could he convince her that he was sharing a moment with her and the babies? How could he ever let go?

Jim awoke when someone kicked him. Immediately he realized he'd fallen asleep next to Teresa, his arms wrapped around her, feeling her stomach. It had been his boys who'd kicked him awake.

He checked his watch. It was a little after eight o'clock. He'd overslept, not waking Teresa when he was supposed to. Before he could do that, he needed to make sure she didn't know he'd slept beside her, his hands touching her.

When he didn't move immediately, he examined his reasons. He was very comfortable next to her. He didn't want to let go. He pictured himself sharing his bed with Teresa every night. He was amazed at the emotions that flowed through him at the thought.

Teresa stirred and that forced Jim to move. Then he leaned over and shook her shoulder. "Teresa?"

"Is it time to get up?" she mumbled.

"No, you can sleep longer if you want. I just need to make sure you're thinking clearly. What's your last name?"

"Tyler," she said, never opening her eyes.

"Okay, I'm going to take a shower. Then I'll fix you breakfast." He was fascinated by how beautiful she looked as she slept. Would their babies look like her? Sleep like her, all curled up, feeling safe and happy?

He'd kill anyone who dared to hurt one of them.

That thought stopped him cold. He hadn't realized he felt that way about Teresa. He hadn't *allowed* himself to think about Teresa because he was so afraid of being trapped into something.

Too late.

He and Teresa were linked for all time by their babies. And once he admitted that, he could allow himself to love her.

He did love her.

A smile broke across his face. When he told his brother, Pete would have a good laugh at his expense. Probably everyone had known all along that he loved Teresa—except him and Teresa herself.

Now all he had to do was convince her.

After his shower, Jim prepared breakfast and called his mother. He explained what had happened to Teresa and asked his mother if she could stay with Teresa today while he did some errands for his houseguest.

"I'll be delighted, son. Thank you for asking. What time shall I come?"

"I'm going to awaken her for breakfast. Can you be here in…half an hour?"

"I'll be there."

It amazed him that his mother was so pleased to be helping.

It hadn't occurred to him that she would want to help. He'd always helped her. Maybe she liked the idea of paying him back. Or maybe it was just that she loved Teresa.

He prepared a tray for Teresa and carried it into the bedroom. "You have to wake up now. I have your breakfast here."

Teresa's eyes popped open. "It smells good, but I have to— Oh, I can't walk."

"You need to go to the bathroom? I'll carry you to the door and you can hop on one foot to, uh, take care of business. Will that do?"

"Yes, thank you," she said politely.

After that maneuver, which included putting on a robe, she asked if she could have her breakfast at the table. "It was very sweet of you to prepare a tray, but I think I'll spill things in bed."

"We can do that if you'll keep your foot propped up. Agreed?"

Again she gave a polite response.

Jim carried the tray back to the kitchen. Then he returned and swung Teresa into his arms. He liked the way she grabbed his neck as he carried her. He liked holding her body next to his, too.

"Th-thank you," she muttered, when he put her in the chair and propped her foot on another seat. "I hope my breakfast hasn't gotten cold."

Jim grinned. "It's frozen waffles. If they have, I'll zap them in the microwave again."

"They smell wonderful. Are you going to eat, too?"

"Of course. I wouldn't miss our first breakfast together," he told her with a smile.

Teresa frowned. "Why am I here?"

"Do you remember what happened last night?" He watched her as she suddenly remembered the previous events.

"Mrs. Patterson— Is she all right?"

"Yes. After I carried you to my car, you made me go back and make sure she was all right. Her son was coming to pick her up."

"But she'll eventually come back, won't she?" Her own doubts were evident in her voice.

"I don't think so. Apparently the burglar destroyed everything he didn't steal."

"No!"

"I'm going over in a few minutes to meet a locksmith I called. We have to change the locks on your house since the burglar got your keys last night."

"I remember. I'll take care of it."

"No, you can't. You're not even allowed to be on crutches for several days. I want to go ahead and get it taken care of before he comes back." He looked at her breakfast and realized their discussion was impeding her appetite. "Eat, honey, so you'll be stronger."

She automatically picked up her fork. After taking a bite of waffle and chewing it, she said, "I'll give you a check to pay the locksmith."

He heard a car come to a halt out front. "I forgot to warn you that I asked my mom to come stay with you while I'm gone. Is that all right?"

"Well, yes, but it won't be much fun for her."

"She doesn't mind. But I want you to sleep more if you feel like it. The doctor said it would be good for you."

"I—I don't want to be a bother."

Jim stood after the doorbell rang and bent to kiss Teresa on the lips. Then he said, "You're no bother, sweetheart."

He opened the door for his mother and thanked her for coming, but Evelyn was more concerned with Teresa. She hurried to the kitchen.

"Oh, my poor dear, how are you?" she asked at once.

"I'm fine," Teresa said, looking at Jim for confirmation.

He poured his mother a cup of coffee and set it before her. "I'm going to go fix up the sofa for you," he said to Teresa. "This way you can watch TV if you want."

"Thank you, Jim. And you, too, Evelyn. I'll try not to be a pest."

"Nonsense, dear," Evelyn said. "It's my pleasure."

After Jim straightened out the blanket and pillow on the couch, he returned to the kitchen for Teresa.

"You didn't eat much," he observed. "Are you feeling okay?"

"Maybe I'll finish it later." She gave him a sleepy smile that had him hungering to take her back to bed.

Tamping down those urges, he scooped her up in his arms and carried her to the sofa. For the first time he wished his new house was bigger, so that he could keep her in his arms longer.

He lowered her to the cushions and before he could tell himself not to, he kissed her. Her lips felt so good against his, he kissed her again. Then, without a word, he strode out the front door.

Feeling like a teenager who had just stolen his first kiss, he smiled to himself.

Maybe there was hope for them, after all, he thought. Because Teresa had kissed him back.

You kissed him back? What were you thinking? she asked herself. And in front of his mother?

Maybe it was some residual confusion after hitting her head. Yes, that was it. Or maybe it was because ever since Jim had taken her to his house, he'd been so attentive, so concerned, so…loving.

This morning had been different from any morning she'd ever woken up to. It had been her first morning with Jim. He'd been different, too. Probably because he felt sorry for her. After all, last night hadn't been the best night of her life.

Or had it?

She remembered Jim waking her to see if she was all right. She remembered him asking to feel the babies move. His hand had felt so big, so warm on her belly. She thought he'd joined her in the bed, but surely she was confused again.

And this morning he'd brought her breakfast in bed. No man had ever done that for her, regardless of the reason. Still, it was a great way to start the day.

But it isn't permanent, said a tiny voice inside her head.

She needed to remember that. It wasn't forever.

Grabbing the remote on the coffee table, she put on some mindless morning show, numbing her brain…and her heart.

Jim got to Teresa's house on the west side of town at the same time as the locksmith. He introduced himself to the middle-aged man wearing a fleece vest and a baseball cap embroidered with a pirate's treasure chest sporting a big lock and key. As Jim opened the door, the locksmith peered over his shoulder.

He pushed back his cap and let out a whistle. "Either Miss Tyler's a real bad housekeeper or that burglar's been back here."

Jim stared at the rubble left in the living room. Now he clearly understood Mrs. Patterson's anger last night. And it wasn't even his house. He was only grateful Teresa hadn't come with him.

When the locksmith started to enter the house, Jim held him back. "We can't go in until I call the police."

The locksmith offered to go on to another job and come back later in the afternoon.

"I appreciate that," Jim said. "Here's my cell number. Call me when you're on your way back."

After he phoned the police, Jim called his sister-in-law to break the news.

"Oh, no!" she exclaimed. "Have you told Teresa?"

"No, she's at home with my mom. I'm afraid to tell her just yet. But she obviously can't come back here before it's cleaned up."

"Of course not. Look, it's a slow day here. I'll come help. Just give me a while to take care of a few loose ends and I'll be there."

The police got there a few minutes later. Jim remained outside while they went in, his anxiety building.

"Mr. Schofield?" One of the policemen came back out to the door. "Did Miss Tyler take her car last night?"

Jim shook his head. "She couldn't drive. She sprained her ankle—" Then he realized what the man was asking. "You mean the burglar stole her car?"

"I can't say for sure, but it's not here. Do you know the make and model, or the license plate?"

"No, but I'll get them." He dialed his home number and waited for his mother to answer. When she did, he asked for Teresa.

He'd dreaded telling her about her house, now he had to add the car to the list. "Honey, I'm sorry, but... we think the burglar came back to your house last night and stole your car."

"Oh, no! Did he tear my place apart like he did Mrs. Patterson's?"

Jim tried to be cagey. "I haven't seen all of it. The police won't let me in yet."

"But from what you've seen of it?"

He couldn't lie to her. "It's trashed."

She held it together, but as she gave him the information about the car, he heard the tears in her voice. "Honey, let me talk to Mom."

When Evelyn took the phone, he told her what had happened. "Comfort her as much as you can, Mom. She loved this house."

Evelyn assumed her patented autocratic tone. "You tell those policemen we expect them to catch this horrible man!"

"I will, Mom. Give Teresa a hug for me."

He flipped shut the phone, feeling terrible that he wasn't there to comfort her himself. But there wasn't much time to dwell on that thought, as Tommie arrived with Pete and Tabitha behind her and a fast-food sack in her hand. Ann and Joel pulled up in seconds.

"What are you all doing here?" Jim asked.

"We're family," Ann replied, as if that said everything. Then she shot him a stern look. "You should've taken Teresa to my house last night."

"I have a big house with lots of room, Ann. She's not a problem." Then, sensing a mother's need to be needed, he added, "I just told Teresa about the break-in. She's upset."

"I'll call her right away." Ann was pulling out her cell phone as she spoke.

About that time, a policeman came out of the

house. "You're going to need to make a list of what's been taken. We got some good prints, we think. Would any of your prints be there?"

Jim said, "I haven't been here in three or four weeks."

The rest of them said the same thing.

"She had Mrs. Patterson over last night for dinner," Jim added.

"Okay, we've got Mrs. Patterson's prints. Now we only need Miss Tyler's prints. Where is she?"

"She's at my house. Here's the address," Jim said, having written the address on the back of his business card. "Do you know when you'll go over?"

"We'd like to go now. The sooner the better."

"Okay. Ann? Can you tell Teresa that the police are coming over to take her fingerprints?"

He would've preferred to tell her himself, but at this point that wasn't possible.

Then, they all surged into the house and stood there, stunned by the damage. After a minute, Jim said, "Why don't we box up whatever is in good condition and we can store it all in my garage until she decides what she wants to do. This place will have to be repaired before anyone can live here again."

"Yes," Tommie agreed. "Maybe doing something will make us feel better."

Ann wiped away a tear and agreed with her oldest daughter.

They took a short break for lunch an hour later, but went back to work quickly. The locksmith returned and replaced the locks on the doors.

By the end of the day they were all exhausted, but the belongings that were not torn or ruined in some manner had all been packed up. The trash had been cleared out and some small repairs done. Jim had made arrangements for a carpenter to come the next day. He also arranged for a local mover to bring the boxes and her bedroom furniture and computer and work desk to his house.

As everyone prepared to leave, Jim asked them to come to his house for dinner, but they were all tired.

"Can we have a rain check?" Ann asked.

"Of course you can."

"Are you sure you don't want to send Teresa to my house?" she added.

"No, I don't want to. And it's easier on Teresa. I can just carry her, not make her hop around."

"May we come see her tomorrow night?"

"Of course. She'd enjoy that."

When they'd all departed, Jim called home. He told his mother he was picking up dinner on his way.

Suddenly he couldn't wait to get home. Not to eat the delicious barbecue he anticipated. But to see Teresa.

Teresa had slept most of the day, especially after the bad news about her house. She could hardly bear to think about her well-loved home torn to shreds. It would take her so long to make it livable again.

She was so tired.

"Jim just called, Teresa. He's picking up barbecue for us for dinner. He said you need the protein," Evelyn said with a chuckle. "He's never worried about *me* getting protein."

"That's only because he doesn't want to have to carry me around and have a houseguest all the time."

"Dear child, my son enjoys carrying you around. Any young man would! And as for having a houseguest, I think he's wanted you in this house since he bought it."

Teresa smiled at Evelyn, but she said nothing. Evelyn didn't know her sons as well as she thought she did.

When Teresa heard the garage door go up, she tensed. Jim was home. But she wasn't. She needed to talk him into taking her— She wasn't sure where to go. It would be too difficult to move in with Tommie and Pete because of the stairs. Tabitha didn't have room for her, and Mom, with her job and her upcoming marriage, didn't have the time.

Before she could come up with an alternative, the door opened and Jim came in, carrying several bags. "Good evening, ladies. Your dinner has arrived."

"That's wonderful, dear, but I forgot tonight is my bridge night," Evelyn said suddenly. "Do you mind if I don't stay and eat after all?"

"No, Mom, of course not, if that's what you want to do."

"Well, I do enjoy my bridge."

"Thank you, Evelyn, for staying with me today," Teresa quickly said.

"I quite enjoyed myself, dear. Call if you need me again."

Before either she or Jim could say anything else, Evelyn was out the door.

Jim slowly turned and stared at Teresa. "Looks like it's just the two of us, Teresa."

"Yes," Teresa agreed, but she didn't want to think about what had happened another time they had dinner alone, about five months ago.

Chapter Nine

"Maybe you should call Tommie and Pete and ask them to come join us?" Teresa asked, changing her mind about eating alone with Jim.

He frowned at her. "I think they'd like to be alone together after their day."

"What do you mean?" she asked, frowning.

"Your entire family came to help pack up your house."

"Pack it up? Why? Was *everything* destroyed?"

"I'm afraid most of it was, Teresa, but we saved what we could."

"Did you explain to them where I was?"

"Of course. Your mother was a little put out that you didn't go to her house, but I explained that I had lots of room in my house."

"And she agreed?" Teresa asked.

"Yeah, because she knows this is where you're supposed to be, Teresa. You're having my babies, aren't you?"

"I'm having *our* babies. You make them sound like they're only yours."

Jim stood for a moment with his head down. Then he looked at Teresa. "You're right. *We* are having *our* babies."

"So, what do we do now?" Teresa asked, sounding depressed.

Jim came over and sat down beside her on the couch. "I'm sorry about your house," he said softly.

"It's okay," she said, blinking fast, trying to hold back the tears. It didn't work, of course.

He put his arms around her and she buried her face in his neck. "Don't cry, honey. It will be all right."

"No, it won't! I'm too tired to clean it and fix it before the babies come!" The tears really flowed then.

Jim gave her a minute to cry before he told her. "Teresa, we cleaned it up today and got rid of anything damaged. I've hired a carpenter to come in after everything is brought over here tomorrow. Then, after I check it out, we can hire a painter."

"I can't afford to do all that!" she snapped in a waterlogged voice.

"But I can. And I'll do it if that's what it takes to make you happy. Now, I'm going to set the table for dinner. And you have to eat twice as much to make up for Mom going home."

She blew her nose with the tissue he gave her.

"You're just saying that to make me feel better," she accused.

"Can't fool you, can I?" He bent down and kissed her before he went to the kitchen.

Teresa watched him over the back of the couch. She hadn't ever seen him so lighthearted. He'd always seemed on his guard, tense. For the first time, tonight he seemed more like his brother. More open.

"It—it must've been hard work today," she said tentatively.

"It was, yeah, but there were a lot of us there. That helped. You've got a nice family, honey. And they all love you."

"I know. But your family is nice, too. It's just a little smaller."

"True. You and Tommie have changed Mom. She used to think only about herself."

"I think she was lonesome. Sometimes it's hard to tell a man your problems. Especially one you're kin to."

"If you marry me, I'll listen to your problems, I promise."

He threw her a teasing grin over his shoulder.

Of course he was teasing. Or she was wanting to read too much into his behavior.

"I suppose you'll understand our boys more than me."

He stopped putting the dishes on the table. "I don't think so. At least not until they reach the teenage years."

"Why would you say that?" Teresa asked.

"Those are the problem years. You've been a kindergarten teacher. I bet you understood both sexes when you were teaching."

"Yes, but I don't know about twins."

"You know about triplets. It's pretty much the same," he assured her with a smile and began again to put the plates in place.

When he set out two containers, Teresa asked, "What are those?"

"Potato salad and green beans. I want to make sure you eat your veggies," he added with a teasing smile.

"I love vegetables, Jim. You don't have to worry."

He left the kitchen and came to the sofa. "I know. You'll do anything for your—check that, *our* babies." Then he bent down and kissed her. Before she could say anything, he picked her up and headed for the breakfast table.

Once they were both seated, Jim began passing her food to fill her plate. "You bought a lot," Teresa said.

"I figured we could eat sandwiches tomorrow for lunch."

"That's true. I love barbecue sandwiches."

"Me, too," Jim returned. He smiled across the table. "Isn't it amazing how many things we have in common?"

"You mean because we both like barbecue? It's Texas, Jim. Everyone loves barbecue."

"And hamburger pizza with extra cheese?" he asked.

"What about hamburger pizza with extra cheese?"

"You don't remember last night?"

"Yes, I…think."

"Pete and Tommie brought over pizza. It was hamburger with extra cheese, your favorite. Which is also my favorite."

Teresa looked a little flustered. "That doesn't prove anything!"

"Just that we have a lot in common," Jim pointed out casually.

"My favorite color is blue!"

"Mine, too."

"I—I hate football!"

"But you love baseball, just like me."

"Stop it! You're not making sense. Those things don't matter!" Teresa protested.

"Calm down, Teresa. I just thought they were interesting observations. It's not important. Eat your dinner."

Teresa stared at him, not sure what to do. She was hungry, actually. Perhaps she should take his advice and eat so the babies would be satisfied. With a cautious eye on Jim, she took a forkful of potato salad.

"Good," he said softly.

She lifted her gaze, prepared to argue with him, but he was concentrating on his dinner. She decided to do the same.

After dinner, Jim put her on the sofa and turned on a reality show. He discovered Teresa had watched it before, as he had. "Another similarity," Jim said.

"I'm not sure. Sometimes I feel like I'm watching a car wreck."

He put her feet in his lap as he sat down. "I know, but it's hard to resist."

They watched the television for several hours. Then Jim took Teresa to the bedroom. "Do you need any help getting ready for bed?"

She looked puzzled. "No, I don't think so."

"Well, I can take you to the door of the bathroom," Jim suggested.

"Okay. Can I take a shower?"

Jim grinned. "Not unless you want me to share it with you."

She gave him a shocked look.

He immediately explained. "You couldn't stand on one leg long without something to lean on. And you can't get your stitches wet, either."

"But I have to wash my hair. How am I going to do that?"

"Hmm, we might be able to figure out a way. Maybe before everyone comes over tomorrow night."

"What are you talking about?"

"Everyone's coming to dinner tomorrow night. I invited them to thank them for their hard work."

"But I can't cook! What will we feed them?"

"I'll order something in. Don't worry about it."

"But we can't—"

He kissed her again. "Take a deep breath, honey. We'll figure out something. Now, in you go. And be careful," he added as he set her down on the floor by the bathroom door.

Teresa took her time in the bathroom. She felt as if she needed some time to herself. Jim had been both friendly and overwhelming this evening. She had so seldom been alone with him, she wasn't sure how to react to him. Besides, he deserved to wait. Inviting her entire family over when she couldn't even walk around? It would be awful if the food was terrible. She'd be so embarrassed.

A sharp rap on the door made her jump, which wasn't good since she was standing one-legged at the sink. Catching her balance, she returned, "What?"

"I was afraid you'd gone to sleep in there."

"No, I haven't," she said as she opened the door.

Without speaking, he swung her up into his arms. "Are you going to be able to dress yourself?"

"I've been able to since I was two, thank you."

He chuckled as he sat her down on the bed. "You know what I mean. Don't sass me."

"Will you really figure out a way for me to wash my hair tomorrow?" she asked after a minute of silence.

"Yes, I will. Now, can you turn off the lamp when you've finished undressing and want to go to sleep?"

"Yes, of course. Are you going in to work tomorrow?"

"No, I don't have time for work," he said, a broad smile on his face.

"Good night, Mr. Smart Alec."

"Good night, my love. Sweet dreams."

She didn't move for several minutes after he closed the door. His gentle teasing left her confused. And lonesome. It reminded her too much of the night they'd made love and made her hunger for his touch. She couldn't afford to let those feelings take hold of her, especially when she was going to live in his house for a few more days.

With a sigh, she put on her nightgown.

When Jim got up the next morning, he immediately called his mother to tell her they were having family night at their house that night. And he asked her for the number of her caterers.

"Of course, dear. When are you going to use them?"

"I just told you, Mom. Tonight when we have everyone over for dinner." He loved the thought of him and Teresa entertaining as a couple.

"Jim, they don't work on that short a notice!" Evelyn told her son.

"They don't?" Jim asked, surprised. "What are we going to do, then?"

"I don't know, dear."

"Okay, I'll—I'll call you later."

He hung up the phone, wondering what he could do now. He supposed he could buy barbecue again, but he didn't think Teresa would be happy.

Pondering his problems, he almost didn't hear Teresa call his name.

He hurried back to his bedroom. He hadn't visited it during the night, since he had no excuse to do so and was too tempted. He gave a quick rap on the door and opened it. "You up already, honey? I thought you'd sleep a little longer."

"Did I wake up at an inconvenient time?"

"Why would you ask that?" Jim asked, avoiding her gaze.

"Well, one reason would be because you won't look at me," Teresa said with a chuckle. "It's a sure sign with kindergarteners. And the other was you seemed out of breath."

"I, uh, just talked to my mother."

Teresa waited a moment. Then she said, "Yes?"

"She's always talking about how this caterer she uses is so wonderful, and I assumed I could just call them and they'd come fix dinner tonight. But she said you have to give them at least two weeks' notice."

"I would imagine that's true."

"But everyone is coming to dinner tonight. What are we going to do?"

"Let's take things one step at a time. Do you have breakfast fixed?"

"I made coffee, but—"

"Do you have any oatmeal?"

"Yeah. Mom bought it for me. She said it was good for me." Jim made a face, which either told Teresa what he thought of oatmeal or of his mother.

"Then take me to the kitchen and lets eat."

Once they were seated at the breakfast table with bowls of oatmeal in front of them, Teresa complimented him. "This is good!"

"How hard is it to make oatmeal? It's not like I can serve that for dinner tonight." He actually let himself laugh and Teresa relished how the smile lit up his hazel eyes.

As much as Jim was fretting about the dinner party, she was looking forward to it. It would be nice to have her family over, except what would she do with her hair?

After they loaded the dishwasher, she asked Jim, "Did you figure out how I can wash my hair?"

He nodded and looked so proud of himself. "You can lie down on the cabinet and *I'll* wash your hair."

Teresa stared at him in stunned silence.

"It will work, honey, I promise."

She pulled at her robe. "I have to get dressed first."

"Are you sure? Won't it get your clothes wet?"

"Not if you do it right."

He mock-saluted her. "Yes, ma'am." Then he gathered her in his arms again and headed for the bedroom.

Fifteen minutes later, with Teresa dressed in jeans and a colorful T-shirt, Jim put her on the long expanse of counter.

"Okay, the water is warm enough. Scoot down a little more and hold that pad over your stitches." He watched as Teresa did as he'd ordered. A shining mass of golden hair fell into the sink. Teresa had unbraided it while she dressed.

Jim had been dying to run his fingers through it. Now he had the opportunity. And it brought back the memory of making love to Teresa. He'd unbraided her hair that night and run his fingers through it. It had felt like liquid gold. Ever since, she'd always had it braided.

He took his time shampooing her hair and then adding cream rinse and washing it out, too. He could spend hours doing this.

"Jim? Aren't you finished?" Teresa asked.

"Oh, yeah. Here, I'll wrap your hair in a towel and then you can sit up." He did as he'd said and then pulled her to a sitting position.

She immediately unwrapped her hair and began rubbing it dry.

"Here, I'll do that. In fact, let me carry you to the sofa and I'll go get my hair dryer."

Before she could agree, Jim scooped her up and carried her to the den. He set her down and promised to be right back.

Almost before she was ready, he was back with his hair dryer and a comb. "Start combing while I plug this thing in," he said and handed her the comb.

"Jim, this really isn't necessary. I can dry my hair by myself."

"I'm enjoying it," he said, taking the comb back and running it through her hair, drying the strands as he lifted them.

"But it's taking too long. We have a lot to do."

"What are you talking about?" He leaned forward to see her face.

"We have to do grocery shopping and cooking for this evening."

Jim stared at her. "I figured I'd go buy some more barbecue."

"I refuse to host that kind of party!" she exclaimed.

"But, honey, you can't cook if you can't stand, and except for oatmeal I'm not exactly handy in the kitchen."

"I'll make a shopping list for you, if you'll bring me a pen and paper."

Jim was frowning ferociously as he brought her what she requested. In the meantime, she'd braided her long hair, still wet.

"Hey, I was going to do that!"

"What?" she asked in surprise.

"I wanted to braid your hair."

His words surprised her…and embarrassed her. "It's all done. Sorry."

As if realizing he'd embarrassed her, he switched subjects. "So what do you think we're going to have for dinner?"

"I think lasagna, tossed green salad, garlic bread and cheesecake for dessert."

"And who is going to make all of it?"

"I'll make the lasagna, you'll make the salad and the garlic bread, and the bakery will make the cheesecake."

"You're kidding!" Jim protested. "I'm an absolute klutz in the kitchen."

"Don't worry, big guy, I'll walk you through it. Now, first of all, we have to see if you have enough dishes."

"You're serious? Teresa—"

"We're wasting time, Jim. How many glass baking dishes do you have? We'll need two."

"I don't have any," he said, looking at her.

"Then you'll have to buy two. Do you have a nice salad bowl?"

"No."

"What *do* you have in your kitchen?"

"Not much, I'll admit. After all, I was just a bachelor," Jim said with a grin.

Teresa suddenly turned away. "Of course. I'm sorry. I wasn't thinking. Just go buy some barbecue and some disposable plates. That will be fine." She put down the pen and paper on the coffee table.

Jim sat down beside her. "Wait! What happened? You don't think I can do this?"

"Jim, it's not a question of whether we can do it. It would be horribly expensive to buy what you need to entertain. It'll be simpler to take out barbecue and paper plates."

"You mean you're acting like this because you're worried about the cost?"

"Yes. I—I sometimes get carried away."

He leaned over and put his finger under her chin, forcing her face up so that he could see her.

"Honey, I don't care about the cost. I'll let you know if I run out of money. But I'd like this house to become a home. A home where you're comfortable. I want us to serve lasagna tonight."

"Are you sure?" she asked.

He picked up the pen and paper she'd set aside. "I'm sure. Keep making your lists. I'll go buy whatever you want."

She wrote down dishes and glasses, serving pieces and linens. When she was done, she handed him the pad.

"Okay. I'll go buy all these things while you make out a grocery list." He stood to go. "Now, do you have everything you'll need while I'm gone?"

"Yes, thank you, Jim."

"I'm not sure what you're thanking me for, but I'm

enjoying myself," he assured her with a kiss. "I'll be back as soon as I can."

He hurried out to the garage, leaving a breathless Teresa on the couch.

The rest of the day, they worked as a team, Jim supplying the legs and Teresa the brain. She gave him instructions on how to prepare for dinner. She sat at the breakfast table, putting together two pans of lasagna, while he made the salad.

Next he prepared the two long loaves of bread with butter and garlic and wrapped them in foil. Then set the table with a blue tablecloth the saleslady had sold him to go with his blue dishes.

"Is that it?" he asked in surprise. "Everything's done?"

"Yes, thanks to you." Teresa had enjoyed their working together. She so much wanted Jim to love her, to share their children, to make a life together.

"But I thought— I mean, Tommie and Pete make entertaining seem so difficult!"

"Well, it helps if someone knows how to cook," Teresa pointed out with a grin.

"Ah, I see. No wonder this was easy. Now, do you want to take a nap before everyone starts to arrive?"

They were interrupted by a knock on the front door.

"That can't be any of our guests," Jim said as he hurried to the door.

When he saw the truck parked at the curb, he remembered what else he had scheduled that day. "Oh, yes. Do you want to come around to the garage?

Most of the boxes will be stored there, and you can bring the furniture into the house that way."

The driver agreed and hurried to get back in his truck. Jim came back to the den and went toward the garage.

"Jim? What is it?" Teresa asked.

"Your things are here. I'm going to store them in the garage, but I'll have your bed set up in one of the bedrooms. That way I won't have to sleep on the sofa."

Reality came back to hit Teresa in the face. Here she'd been thinking—hoping—for a future with Jim as his wife, his beloved wife, but he was temporarily storing her things and setting up her bed so he could have his own back.

She had to remember she was only a temporary guest in Jim Schofield's home.

Chapter Ten

Jim sensed a change in Teresa's attitude the minute he returned to the den. She was sitting on the sofa, her shoulders hunched, her head down.

"Teresa, is anything wrong?"

"No, of course not," she said quickly. But even the glimmer in her eye that he'd seen during their dinner preparations moments ago was gone, replaced by a dimness that he couldn't quite identify. Before he could pursue it, she asked, "Will my things fit in the garage?"

He nodded. "If you had a car, we'd be tight, but..." He trailed off when he saw her sad expression. "The cops have my number. Maybe they'll call tomorrow."

"Maybe," she agreed, but her tone didn't show much hope.

Was that it? He wondered. Was she feeling trapped here without a car? Maybe all she needed to pick up her spirits was a day or two out of the house. "I can take you wherever you want to go. And you can drive in a few days when your ankle's better."

When she didn't reply, he tried another approach. "Would you like your desk set up in one of the spare bedrooms? I have three of them." One of them he'd already dubbed the babies' room, though he'd yet to show her. He wasn't sure she'd like it. Besides, they had other things to settle before they worried about a room for their sons. "This way you can write whenever you'd like."

That at least got a response out of her. "That'd be fine. Maybe after everyone leaves tonight, I can work awhile."

He turned on the TV, hoping there was something on to amuse her. She still seemed unhappy.

Within an hour, her bedroom was set up, except for sheets on the bed. Teresa asked Jim about them, and he confessed the burglar had taken a knife to the bed linens. He hadn't thought to buy any others.

"I can go buy you some, though."

"Why don't I call Tommie and see if she has any to fit my bed? That will save time." Teresa reached for the phone.

Jim watched her, wondering if that was what they should do. *He* wanted to be the one to supply Teresa with everything she needed.

Tommie promised Teresa she would bring what her sister needed when they came for dinner.

Jim went into the bedroom set aside for Teresa. He took her clothes out of the suitcase and hung them up so they wouldn't be so wrinkled. Not that he'd ever done that before, but he wanted to see her things unpacked, so he could believe she *lived* there.

"Jim? What are you doing?"

He spun around, staring at Teresa. He'd left her on the sofa. "How'd you get there? Did you hop down the hall? You shouldn't do that, you know. You might hurt yourself more."

"I'm fine. I wanted to see what— This is a nice room."

"Yeah. Look at the window seat."

Jim didn't realize what he said until she began hopping across the room. He jumped to help her and ended up colliding with her, the two of them tumbling to the window seat.

"I'm sorry, honey. I was trying to help you."

Awkwardly she pushed herself upright. "No harm, no foul." She leaned back against the wall and looked around the room. "I think you've unpacked everything that needs to be hung up. The rest is… personal."

Jim looked at the suitcase and realized it held only underwear and nightgowns. "Oh, uh, yeah."

"I—I think I'll rest a little while and then change for dinner."

"You mean dress up?" he asked in surprise.

"No, just something nicer than jeans and a T-shirt."

"Okay, but you look good in what you have on." He gave her a big smile.

Teresa said nothing, apparently just waiting for him to leave.

"I'll call you about six-thirty. Everyone's coming at seven," he added, watching her.

"Thank you," she said softly.

That was as much as he was going to get, he decided, and backed his way out of her room.

The nap did her good.

She dressed in red jersey slacks and a matching sweater, one of the few maternity outfits she'd bought.

She rebraided her hair and took her time with her makeup. But, checking her watch, she realized she still had over half an hour until everyone arrived. Too much time to be alone with Jim. Why not look at her "office" he had set up for her? She wasn't sure which bedroom he'd chosen, but they were both at the other end of the hall.

When she opened the first door, her heart stopped. Here was the perfect nursery, already set up for her babies. She was stunned that Jim had gone to so much trouble for his sons.

The cribs were white with blue gingham bedding over pale-blue sheets. Above each hung a mobile with colorful dancing bears and ponies.

The walls were done in a blue wash, and puffy clouds floated on the ceiling.

It was the nursery of her dreams.

She hopped a little farther into the room until she reached the two little dressers. Opening one drawer, she found several outfits in pale colors, each one so tiny she could hardly believe a human being would fit them. She fingered their softness and felt an overwhelming sense of anticipation. How could she possibly wait for the twins to be born?

Jim had done all this?

She wasn't aware she was crying until he called her name. He hurried to her side and wiped her cheeks.

"Why are you crying, sweetheart?" he asked softly. "Don't you like it?"

"I—I— It's so perfect! It's how I dreamed, but I never could've— You did all this?"

"Yeah, with Mom's help. I didn't really know what we'd need, but I wanted to be prepared. I hoped to convince you to marry me and I wanted to have everything ready for our babies."

Teresa remembered her conversation with Mrs. Patterson. Her dear friend had said it would be best for her babies if their father was with them, too. More than anything Teresa wanted the best for her babies.

Her tears fell faster now as she realized she was giving up her dream of love for herself. But this room was filled with love for her babies. She couldn't turn that down. She'd be wrong to turn that down.

She drew a deep breath. "All right, Jim, I'll marry you."

For a minute, he didn't seem to understand what she'd said. Wiping her cheeks, he was cuddling her against him and started to tell her again not to cry. But her words registered finally, and he took her by the shoulder and moved her back so he could see her face.

"Did you just say you'd marry me?" he asked in disbelief.

"Yes, if you're still willing," she said slowly, giving him plenty of time to withdraw.

He let out a big sigh of relief. "I'm willing, honey. When?"

"I—I don't know."

"We can talk it over at dinner," he said, enthusiasm in his voice.

"I don't— Jim, we need—"

"What do we need? Don't you want to tell your family? It'll be great. We'll be celebrating our engagement this evening, in our house. Too bad I don't have a ring for you. But we can take care of that tomorrow. I'm sure Mom can organize everything."

He swung Teresa up in his arms and carried her to the den. "This is going to be the best evening ever!"

Teresa feared it was going to be the worst.

She was engaged and she hadn't even been kissed.

"We're getting married."

That was how Jim greeted everyone who came for dinner. Tommie and Pete were the first to arrive.

Thrilled with the news, they rushed into the living room to hug Teresa.

Teresa returned the embrace, but couldn't manage any words past the lump in her throat. Her sister must have sensed something, because when Tommie pulled back, her big smile was replaced by an odd look. Skepticism.

Tommie knew something was up. After all, Teresa thought, you didn't share a womb with someone and not be attuned to their emotions.

But before Tommie could ask, the doorbell rang with the next arrivals, who mobbed the newly engaged couple. Tommie excused herself to go put the linens on Teresa's bed, leaving her to face Tabitha, her mother and Joel, and then Evelyn.

To everyone, Teresa smiled the right smile, but she spoke only to Evelyn, thanking her for the boys' nursery.

"It was a pleasure, my dear. I'm so happy we're all going to be one big happy family."

Ann Tyler took her aside and asked her softly, "This is what you want, isn't it, Teresa?"

"Yes, Mom." She forced her smile to reach her eyes. "You've got to get Evelyn to show you the nursery. It's perfect." Then she asked Jim to take her to the kitchen, where they got dinner on the table.

As the night wore on, Teresa could feel her emotions sinking like a lead weight through water, drifting slowly but inexorably to the bottom. She might have made her decision to marry Jim, but she'd never understood how hard it would be to live up to her resolve. Until now.

By the time dinner was over, she had plans to shop for her wedding gown with Evelyn, to meet with caterers and to line up potential florists. Without her saying a word, her entire week was packed solidly with meetings and preparations for a wedding that was suddenly scheduled for the next Sunday, only ten days away.

Jim had been so caught up in the lively discussions that he hardly noticed how perfectly he'd fit the role of host, serving lasagna, refilling glasses. When Evelyn complimented Teresa on the dinner, she couldn't accept the praise, instead deflecting it where it truly belonged. "Jim deserves the congratulations."

"Well, thanks, but you're the one who made it all work. You're a great cook."

"You're not going to get any argument from us," Joel agreed, speaking on behalf of everyone assembled.

His words brought genuine pleasure to Teresa for the first time that night.

Jim stood up. "Now it's cleanup time. And since I do know how to do that, you can all go into the den while I do the dishes."

The women all insisted on helping, and together they accomplished the chore in no time. Teresa was grateful. She was exhausted, even though she hadn't done the work herself. Dealing with all the emotional happenings of the day had left her wiped out.

Her mother seemed to notice it, and suggested they all leave so that Teresa could rest.

At once, everyone got to their feet, thanked her for the dinner and reiterated what they would be doing for her wedding.

Teresa made her goodbyes and while Jim was escorting them out, she hopped to her room and closed the door behind her.

She couldn't bear any more congratulations.

A rap on the door had her looking up from the bed where she'd collapsed. "Honey?"

"Yes, Jim, I'm fine. Just tired. I'm going to bed."

"Don't you need me to help you, uh, get around?"

"No, thank you."

"You haven't changed your mind, have you?"

She heard the panic in his voice. It was tempting to tell him she was wavering, but that wouldn't be fair. "No, I haven't changed my mind."

"Everything is going to be great, honey. You'll see."

"Yes. I'll see you in the morning."

"After you get settled, I may go into the office, if you don't need me."

"That will be fine." At least she would have time to breathe and shore up her determination.

It took Jim some time to wind down from the excitement of the engagement. He couldn't believe he was going to have his family after all.

Now he knew he could take care of Teresa and his boys, provide for them. His future was set. He loved her and hoped their marriage could become a real one, but he was learning to be patient.

He'd been prepared to pursue Teresa until the babies were born. But, as Pete had said, he didn't want to be excluded from the delivery room when it was time. He wanted to see his boys at once, not introduced to them later, like a nice uncle.

And that was why he was willing to be patient. He'd accomplished one goal. He'd work on the second—making Teresa his real wife—when she'd gotten used to having him around. Maybe by then he wouldn't even have to confess his love for her. She'd just know.

He didn't want to spend much time examining his reasons for not wanting to tell her. Suffice to say that loving someone made him feel weak, vulnerable. Admitting that love…well, he'd try to avoid it.

Just thinking about that potential conversation made him jumpy and set him to pacing around the den as he watched the news. After the sports, he went to bed to read. But when he crawled into bed, he caught the faint lingering scent that was intrinsically Teresa. He threw the book to the floor. There was no point even trying to concentrate on anything other than that scent.

He'd just lie back and wrap himself in her smell and remember the night they'd made love, the night they'd made two little babies. That night he'd like to repeat over and over again.

When Teresa reached the kitchen the next morning, she found Jim there making breakfast. "Can I give you a hand?" she asked.

He shook his head. "Got it all under control. Besides, why didn't you call me to come and get you? You shouldn't be hopping around." He took the skillet off the stove and spooned scrambled eggs into two plates already holding country sausages and biscuits. "All ready."

Teresa sat down, grateful for the distraction of the big breakfast. This way she wouldn't have to talk much to Jim, especially about last night.

"When do you get your stitches out?"

She jerked her head up. "Uh, I'll ask someone when I go to the hospital to get a pair of crutches."

"I forgot about that. I'll rearrange my schedule so I can take you."

"No. Your mother said she would take me there before we went shopping." She looked at him quickly, then stared again at her eggs.

"Okay, if you're sure of that," he said slowly, watching her.

"Yes, we talked about it last night."

"All right, then, I'll go get dressed for the office."

She merely nodded, then let out a sigh when he hurried to his bedroom. She hopped to the sink and rinsed her dish, leaning against the counter. Afterward, she went to the sofa and sat down, ready to kill an hour or two before Evelyn came to pick her up.

Jim came through the den but, with his mind on work, never even saw her there, until she called, "Have a nice day."

He looked up in surprise, then offered her the same wish. "I should be home around five," he called over his shoulder on his way to the garage.

Once she heard the garage door go down, she closed her eyes. She was finding that any time spent around Jim was difficult and took a lot of energy.

All those casual kisses he'd given her before she'd agreed to marry him had stopped. And that told her more than anything that he wasn't attracted to her, only to his boys.

What had she done?

The ringing of the telephone distracted her. Fortunately, the phone was within her reach.

"Miss Tyler?" a deep voice asked.

"Yes."

The caller identified himself as Mr. Brown, an agent from her insurance company.

"We need to discuss your claims for your house and car. We just got word that the police have found your vehicle. Had you heard?"

"No, I hadn't! I'm thrilled. When will I get it back?"

"I'm sorry, but you won't. We're considering it a total loss."

Teresa was disappointed. "What—what happens now?"

"We'll give you the book value. We also have a check for your belongings and for the repairs that must be made in your house." He named an amount Teresa thought was fair. She agreed to it and the amount for the car.

"Good," the agent said. "Will you be home this morning? I can bring you the check and papers to sign."

"I'm at my—my fiancé's house." She gave him the address, feeling strange using that word.

"I'll be there in an hour," he promised.

She barely hung up the phone when it rang again.

This time it was Jim. When she told him the news and the amounts she'd agreed to, he barked, "I'm on my way home. Don't sign anything until I get there!"

She hung up the phone wondering what he was upset about.

Chapter Eleven

His protective instincts were kicking in. Flexing their muscles like bodybuilders on the beach. He knew he was being obnoxious, but couldn't stop himself.

The car jolted to a stop in his driveway and he barged in, calling, "Teresa?"

"We're in the living room," she returned.

He hurried in and eyed the tall, middle-aged stranger standing there with his hand outstretched. "I'm Mr. Brown from Miss Tyler's insurance company. You must be Mr. Schofield."

Jim shook the proffered hand, but didn't keep the edge out of his voice. "I want to evaluate the sum you've come up with for reimbursement. I know how insurance adjusters can be."

"Jim!" Teresa protested. "I think the estimates are fair."

The adjuster picked up the papers from the coffee table. "As long as it's okay with you, Miss Tyler, we can let Mr. Schofield see them."

Teresa hesitated, and Jim could practically see the wheels turning in her head. He knew he'd embarrassed her, but would she see that he was only looking out for her? Finally she nodded and Jim took the papers.

After he examined the totals, he calmed down. "These seem to be in line, Mr. Brown. Uh, sorry, I acted…"

"No need to apologize," the agent said. He instructed Teresa where to sign the papers, then handed her a check for the bottom line. "Again, Miss Tyler, I'm sorry for your trouble." After shaking her hand, he let Jim show him out.

When Jim reentered the living room, he walked right into trouble.

"I've got a news flash for you, Jim. Being pregnant didn't make me stupid." Her tone was angry, her demeanor cold.

Trying to crack through the ice, he started apologizing.

"I'm sorry, I—"

"Don't. You should probably just get back to work." She turned away and starting hopping out of the room.

Letting out a frustrated growl, he picked her up in one quick motion. "Where do you want to go?"

"I was going to the den to wait for your mother,"

she said, trying to catch her breath and keep her arms crossed over her chest so as not to touch him.

"How about the kitchen? We can have something to drink while we wait."

"Fine."

After he set her down, he poured two glasses of orange juice. "This'll be good for the babies."

"Should I drink both glasses, one for each baby?" she asked, deadpan.

"Nope. One's for me. They'll just have to share. Might as well learn young."

Finally Teresa let show a glimmer of a smile, and it was exactly what Jim wanted. He needed to know they were okay, that he hadn't irreparably offended her by his brutish behavior.

When she said nothing else, he asked, "What are you planning to do with the insurance money?"

"I thought I'd use it to repair the house. I've got to pay the carpenter and the painters."

"Then what? Rent it out?" He hoped she didn't think he was prying, but he needed to know.

"I...I don't know yet, to be honest." She didn't look at him.

"Well, it's up to you." Just then he heard a car door shut. Thankful for the distraction, he said, "I can't believe it. Mom's here on time."

When he let Evelyn in, he grabbed his keys and left, tossing over his shoulder, "See you tonight, Teresa."

Teresa thought Evelyn looked a bit miffed that her son hadn't fussed over her. But the older woman said nothing of the kind, just prompted Teresa to get ready. "We have appointments, dear."

"I'm all set." But their departure was interrupted by the ringing phone.

Tommie dispensed with pleasantries and cut to the chase. "Teresa, what are you going to do with your house?"

Why was everyone suddenly so interested in her little place? She thought. "I don't know. As a matter of fact, I got the insurance check just a few minutes ago."

"One of the agents in my office has a client looking for a house near Texas Christian University for his two sons. Are you interested in selling?"

Was she? She wouldn't need the house, what with living at Jim's. But, she admitted honestly, it was nice to have, as a safety net. Maybe that wasn't the best attitude to have going into a marriage…. "But the repairs haven't even been finished on the place, Tommie."

"I've explained all that, but the guy's into fixer-uppers. Just think, Teresa, you could bank the entire settlement. For the twins."

That was exactly what Teresa needed to hear. "Fine, let's do it. I'll bring you a key in a few minutes."

They added that chore to the long list ahead of them, checking off one by one as the day progressed. Some were tedious, like ordering flowers; some were enjoyable, like choosing the wedding cake, which she got to taste-test. Others were just plain necessary, like stopping at the hospital to get her crutches. The nurse there said her stitches could probably come out in a few days.

"I hope so," Teresa said when they'd gotten back in the car. "Or I'll look like a bride, all right. The Bride of Frankenstein."

Evelyn chuckled, then soothed her, "Don't worry, dear. You're going to be a beautiful bride."

"And you're going to be a great mother-in-law."

"Of course I am. And why not? I love my sons, as do you and Tommie, so we have a lot in common." When Teresa said nothing, Evelyn prodded, "You do love Jim, don't you?"

Love Jim?

Yes, despite his sometimes overbearing actions, like this morning, she loved him. With all her heart.

"Yes," she whispered, "I do."

Evelyn beamed at Teresa. "That's wonderful. Now, I think we have time for the most important thing. Buying your wedding gown."

"Mom said she would—"

"I know she would, Teresa, but she has her own wedding to pay for. I want to buy your gown for you. Please?"

"Of course, Evelyn, if you want to, but I could pay for it with my insurance check."

"No, you need to invest that. A woman needs some of her own money."

Since they'd put it in the teacher's credit union first thing that morning, Teresa knew it was already drawing interest. "Are you sure we have time to go shopping today?"

"Most definitely. I called the wedding gown co-ordinator at Neiman's and she agreed to wait for us."

"But Neiman's is so expensive, Evelyn!"

"Yes, but they're so nice," Evelyn assured her as she pulled into the parking lot. "Shall I let you out at the door? Then I'll go park."

Teresa stood by the door, waiting for Evelyn. She hoped Evelyn wouldn't spend too much. She was sure they could find a cheaper dress some-where else.

Evelyn caught up with her and led the way to Neiman's bridal salon. "Mrs. Peters? I'm Evelyn Schofield. I talked to you earlier."

"Hello, Mrs. Schofield. I'm so pleased you could make it. And this is—"

"My future daughter-in-law, Teresa Tyler."

"Oh, she's beautiful! But will you be on crutches for the wedding?"

"I hope not," Teresa said with a smile. "And my stitches should come out beforehand also."

"Oh, good. Shall we get started? What size are you?" the woman asked.

Teresa's cheeks flushed, but she said, "I was an eight, but now I'm five months pregnant with twins."

"Congratulations." Mrs. Peters gave her a genu-ine smile. "But not to worry. I think we can disguise that a little. I know just the gowns."

Teresa had her doubts, but when they found the perfect dress, she had to admit it was true. The only hitch was the price, but Evelyn assured her that wasn't a problem.

They got to Jim's house late, and he heated up lasagna and made another salad. They even had cheesecake for dessert.

"We may have to throw out the rest of that cheesecake, if we don't finish it tonight," Teresa said.

Jim frowned. "Does it go bad that fast?"

"No, but I don't need the calories if I'm to fit in my gown on Sunday."

"I suspect you burned a lot of calories today, so I wouldn't worry about it," he said with a smile.

The three of them cleaned up, returning the kitchen to its pristine condition. Evelyn asked when the cleaning lady came, and Jim said, "This coming Friday. I may have to ask her to start coming every week instead of every other week."

"You have a cleaning lady?" Teresa asked in surprise.

"Yeah. But we'll need her more often," Jim said.

"I can take care of the house."

Jim and Evelyn smiled at Teresa. Finally, Jim said, "Honey, you're going to get much larger and cleaning house will be hard on you."

"But—but it will be my job. Of course I can do it."

They smiled at her and went on with their conversation.

Teresa wondered what Jim would get out of this marriage if he didn't want sex or housekeeping. Of course, she realized. His babies. That had always been what he wanted. She had nothing else to contribute to the marriage, in Jim's mind.

She almost told Evelyn to take the wedding gown

back to the store, but she reminded herself she was not marrying Jim for herself. She was marrying him for her babies.

Before she went to bed that night, she slipped into the nursery. Quietly standing there she absorbed the love in the room. Love that she would claim for her sons. If not for herself.

Their wedding day was approaching much faster than Teresa could believe—and much more slowly than she'd thought possible.

There was so much to do, she didn't have time to think. But there were rare quiet moments as well. In those moments, when fear filled her heart, she didn't think she could go through with the marriage.

One such moment was when Mrs. Patterson called her. "Teresa, is that you?"

"Mrs. Patterson, where are you?"

"I'm at my son's house. Are you all right?"

"Oh, yes. I'm on crutches for another day or so, and I have stitches, but they're coming out soon."

"I'm so glad. I should've called earlier, but I've been settling in here."

"Is it going well?"

"Better than I ever imagined. My grandsons can now come straight home after school. I feed them a snack and help them with their homework. Oh my, I'm learning a lot, I must say."

"You sound very happy, Mrs. Patterson."

"Oh, I am, my dear. It's nice to feel needed."

"Yes. I'm glad to know you're happy."

"What about you? Have you made any decisions?"

Teresa knew exactly what Mrs. Patterson was referring to. "Yes, I'm going to marry Jim."

"He seemed like a nice man, and handsome, too."

"Yes, he is," Teresa said. "Mrs. Patterson, I'd love to have you at the wedding." She gave her all the details.

"Look, dear, I must go make the after-school snack for my grandsons. Call me if you want to talk," Mrs. Patterson said, giving Teresa her number. "And I think you're doing the right thing."

"Thank you. I'll see you at the wedding."

"I wouldn't miss it."

The morning of the wedding, Teresa was able to walk through the house without her crutches. The house was full of beautiful flowers that had been brought in the day before.

The chairs in the living room were arranged with a center aisle. And in the dining room, across the entryway, the bride's cake and groom's cake sat in isolated splendor. She was staring at them when Jim came down the hall.

"You're up already?" he asked. "Mom said to let you sleep late this morning."

"I didn't want to."

"Come on, the least I can do is fix you breakfast."

"No, I can fix breakfast. I thought I'd make pancakes this morning."

Jim appeared to be involved in a struggle. "I know I shouldn't let you cook, but I do love pancakes."

"Then follow me. You don't even have to carry me this morning."

"Your foot's not hurting you any?"

"No, not at all." She lied, but it wouldn't hurt anything. The doctor had warned her she'd suffer a little discomfort at first.

"Too bad. I kind of liked carrying you around."

She smiled, but said nothing. She certainly couldn't admit how much she'd liked being carried around in his arms. Especially since those were the only times he'd touched her after she agreed to marry him.

"Why don't you put on the coffee for me, please?" she suggested in an attempt to keep him busy.

"Sure, I'll be glad to. Do you miss not drinking coffee?" he asked.

Teresa was mixing the pancake batter and looked up in surprise. "Some, I guess, but hot tea works fine."

"You want me to make some tea for you?"

"I can fix it later," she assured him as she put on some bacon to cook.

He grinned. "Yeah, you could, if you had three arms! I'll fix your tea."

Shortly, the two of them sat down to hot pancakes and crisp bacon. But there was no conversation. Teresa guessed Jim was as reluctant to talk as she was.

When he finished his breakfast, he sat back with a smile on his face. "That was terrific, Teresa. Thank you."

"You're welcome." After a pause, she said, "Jim, are you sure we're doing the right thing?"

"Of course we are. We're going to have a great family, honey. Don't ever doubt it."

She said nothing else as she started stacking the dishes.

"Now, I *know* I'm not supposed to let you do the dishes. Go take a bubble bath or something. Everyone will start arriving in an hour, and the caterers will be here sooner than that. Don't worry if you hear the doorbell. I'll take care of everything."

Jim watched Teresa walk down the hall to her bedroom. He hoped they got through the wedding. He had a feeling something wasn't right, but he wanted to postpone any problems for a few days…or weeks. He believed they just needed a chance to get used to each other.

He counted breakfast this morning as a good start to their marriage. They hadn't had any arguments. They liked the same things. And they both loved their boys. He knew Teresa would be a wonderful mother.

Just thinking about her holding one of her babies brought a smile to Jim's face.

The doorbell put an end to his daydream, announcing the arrival of the caterers. They began setting up at once. The buffet would be served in the den, where tables and chairs filled the room.

"Mr. Schofield? May we have the kitchen?"

Jim looked up to find one of the caterers obviously waiting for him to move out of the way. "Yeah, let me fill my coffee mug and I'll go to my bedroom."

Before he could escape, Pete and Tommie arrived. She went to Teresa's bedroom to see if she could help her get ready, while Pete grabbed a cup of coffee and went to his brother's room with him. Jim stepped into dark suit pants and began buttoning his crisp white shirt.

"Can you believe I'm going to be married, just like you?" he asked.

"I hope you're happy about it."

"Yeah, I am. Teresa is going to make a wonderful mother."

"And wife?" Pete added.

"Sure, that, too."

"Have you told Teresa you love her?" Pete asked sternly.

Poised over the buttons, Jim's hands stilled. Pete knew? Was he that obvious, or did one man in love have the ability to recognize another? Still, he couldn't admit it. The feeling was best secreted away where no one else but he knew of its existence. Instead, he frowned at this brother. "What are you, the marriage police?"

"I'm your brother and I want you to be happy."

"I am happy. Don't worry about me."

Pete shook his head but said nothing else.

When they heard the doorbell again, Jim went to the door and discovered his mother there chatting with the caterers, and making sure they had forgotten nothing.

"Jim, I'm going to make a pitcher of iced tea, if you don't mind," Evelyn called down the hall. Jim assured her that would be fine, since he knew she'd do it anyway. He guessed the caterers were used to having her around.

Evelyn assigned herself the task of official greeter. She opened the door to Tabitha, whom she sent to Teresa's room, then to Ann and Joel to whom she offered iced tea.

"That would be so nice, thank you, Evelyn," Ann said with a smile. "Where's Teresa? I can't wait to see the gown she picked out. I've been meaning to thank you for all the help you've given her."

"Your daughters are such joys, Ann. I've enjoyed every minute of it."

Jim and Pete came into the den at that moment. "Did Tabitha bring a date?" Pete asked.

"No, she didn't. We need to find someone for her, too. It's too bad I don't have another son," Evelyn said with a beaming smile.

The doorbell rang again, and this time it was Mrs. Patterson, with her son. Jim hurried to introduce his mother to Teresa's friend and neighbor, and welcomed them in.

Before he could shut the door, the minister pulled up. After he ushered in the man and his wife, he told Pete, "You want to let the girls know that it's time?"

With a nod, Pete hurried down the hall. He rapped on the door and everyone could hear his low murmur. Then the door opened slightly before it closed again.

Pete came back down the hall. "Okay, they'll be ready in two minutes. So everybody take your places."

Tommie and Tabitha came down the hall and into the living room, smiling at their mother and Joel.

Pete put his arm around his wife. "Everything okay?"

"I hope so," she said.

The recorded music started to play, and the guests turned toward the doorway.

But the bride did not appear.

Chapter Twelve

Tommie got up and hurried back down the hall. She found her sister sitting on the bed in her wedding gown, sobbing.

"Teresa, what's wrong?" she asked, fearing her sister had had a breakdown.

"I can't get my shoes on. I wore these shoes last spring. Why can't I get them on?"

"Here, I'll help you," Tommie said, taking one of the shoes and trying to jam it on her sister's foot. It wouldn't go. Teresa was crying more, saying her foot hurt.

"Just go barefoot, Teresa. Jim won't even notice."

"I can't do that!"

A knock on the door distracted them. Tommie opened it to her mother.

"What's wrong?"

After her daughter's explanation she smiled a mother's knowing smile. "Of course she can't wear those shoes. Her feet are swollen and probably larger than they were. That happened to me. After I was pregnant with you three, my feet went up two sizes. What have you been wearing, Teresa?"

"My tennis shoes," she said, her sobs easing.

"Well, you can either go barefoot or wear your tennis shoes. But right now your fiancé is thinking you don't want to marry him."

Teresa stood, her skirt falling gracefully around her. "Mom, will you go tell Jim I'll be right out? I just want to fix my face."

"Of course I will. We'll restart the music and you come then." Grabbing Tommie by the hand, Ann left the room.

Teresa sat on the bed, wiping her tears away. The shoe fiasco was almost like a sign from God that she was doing the wrong thing. Or was she being silly? After all, she was doing the right thing for her babies.

With a sigh, she stood and opened the door. Down the hall she went, her chin up and a smile on her lips. She walked into the living room, barefoot, and married Jim Schofield, father of her unborn twins.

Except for being barefoot, the wedding was just as Teresa would have wanted it. The cakes were beautiful and tasted even better. Her family and Jim's were there to celebrate with them, even Mrs. Patterson. Jim had hired a photographer to take pictures of their wedding and insisted the man get a picture of her bare feet.

When all their guests and the caterers left, the house felt very lonely. Even more so because her husband was not acting like a newlywed. He was scrupulously polite, suggesting that she take a nap, fixing her a snack of leftovers, treating her like a guest. She would have preferred being treated like a friend, rather than a stranger.

When it was nighttime, and the pretense was over, he sent her to bed in her own bedroom, across the hall from his.

Teresa lay in bed, wondering what she was supposed to do. It was clear now, painfully clear, that he had married her only for the boys. She shouldn't expect a real relationship.

Okay, that was the reason she'd married him, too, to be fair. But she loved him. She'd dreamed of him touching her, holding her close. She'd pictured them sharing warm evenings, watching television, going to movies, doing things couples did.

But she'd been mistaken.

It took a long time to fall asleep, on her wedding night.

Jim tried to blame his sleeplessness on caffeine, but he hadn't had that much coffee. He paced the floors, telling himself he was worried about his work, but he couldn't convince himself of that when visions of Teresa, coming down the abbreviated aisle, her toes peeking out, occupied his mind.

His heart had sunk when she hadn't appeared on cue. He'd been afraid she'd changed her mind. When her mother had told him it was her shoes that were causing the problem, it was a huge relief.

Teresa had made a beautiful bride. He was so glad he'd hired a photographer. At least he could look at the beautiful images. As the day had gone on, Teresa seemed to grow more distant, however.

Maybe it was his fears that had made her seem distant. He hoped their marriage would turn into one like Pete and Tommie's, but he'd thought he shouldn't press her in the beginning.

Tonight that seemed like a bad decision.

But he wasn't only thinking of himself. Teresa deserved some space, some time to adjust to the abrupt change in her life. He didn't want to give in to his own desires and not take her happiness into consideration.

So he'd lose a little sleep. Maybe a lot of sleep, he amended when he looked at the clock. But he'd survive. And hopefully his marriage would, too.

Teresa sat at the breakfast table, trying to decide what to do. She stared into her orange-juice glass as if it contained tea leaves that would direct her future.

They'd been married for two weeks. Two grueling, unhappy weeks. Each day Jim became more polite, more distant. He avoided even the most casual touch. He had taken to working longer hours because he didn't want to come home and face her.

In other words, she was making his life miserable.

So what did she do now? She had the money from the insurance company. And her house had been sold, as is, to the father of the two college boys. When it closed, she would receive another big check. So she had enough money to make it for a while.

She could leave a note for Jim, explaining that she needed some time. She wouldn't tell him she needed the time to make sure she could be around him without showing any emotion. But she would contact him before the babies were born so he'd be there when they entered the world.

And she would promise to share them with him.

She had a lot to do if she was going to pull off her escape without anyone knowing. She began making a list.

It took her several days. She found a used-car lot with a vehicle she was comfortable with. Then she rented an apartment not too far away. She bought a cheery red sleeper sofa, a coffee table and a television and had the delivery set up for two days later.

On her last day in Jim's beautiful house, she baked several items for Jim and froze more lasagna for him. She worried about him eating properly. Then she wrote him a long note of explanation and carried her bags to the front door. She'd arranged for a taxi to come at 2:00 p.m. When it pulled up, she took one last look around the house and carried her bags out to the taxi.

She directed the driver to the used-car lot, where she transferred her bags to her new purchase and headed for the first-floor apartment she'd rented. At four in the afternoon, the delivery truck pulled up with her other purchases.

She was home.

And she cried for hours.

* * *

Jim sat at the office for more than half an hour. He'd finished all the work he could find to do. In fact, he'd been caught up for several days, but he didn't want to go home.

It wasn't that he didn't want to see his bride. Teresa occupied his thoughts most of the day. The wife of one of his partners was expecting, and the guy was constantly telling stories about how difficult she was, with her mood swings and cravings. Jim hadn't quite gotten up the nerve to tell them his wife was pregnant. In fact, he hadn't even told them he was married. He took off his ring each morning and carried it in his pocket until it was time to go home again.

He wanted to tell them everything, especially about his boys. But if he told them about Teresa, invitations would follow. He wasn't sure Teresa would like that.

He wasn't sure about anything when it came to Teresa. He'd been spending less and less time with her because it took so much energy *not* to touch her, *not* to reach for her for even the most casual of reasons. He was going to have to talk to her, to explain his behavior if things didn't change soon.

With a sigh, he got up and headed out the door. Time to face his wife and confess his problem. He loved her. He wanted her. He'd been wrong. Could she ever forgive him?

The house was dark when he got home. Not a good sign. She must've gone to bed early. He moved to the kitchen, clicking on the light.

That was when he saw the paper on the breakfast table with his name on it.

Had he waited too long?

He grabbed the paper and sat down in the chair at the table to read it.

Though he wanted to cry when he'd finished Teresa's letter, he held back. Tears wouldn't help. He had to find her. He called her mother first, sure that was where Teresa had gone.

"No, Jim, Teresa's not here. Have you lost her?" Ann asked with a laugh.

"I must've just thought she said she was going to your house this evening. Probably she's over at Tommie's. Sorry I disturbed you, Ann."

He called Pete and Tommie next. They denied all knowledge of Teresa's whereabouts. He buried his pride and told them Teresa had left him, and he needed to know if she was safe and…and if she'd ever talk to him again.

When Pete relayed that information to Tommie, she grabbed the phone away from him. "You don't know where she is? What did she say?"

"She said she needed time, but she'd contact me before the babies are born so I could be there. Like that was the only thing she thought I wanted."

"You never told her you love her, did you?" Tommie asked accusingly.

"I—I thought I should give her some time to adjust."

"Jim Schofield, I could wring your neck! She's carrying your babies, and you thought you should wait to tell her that you love her? That's crazy!"

He could hear Pete in the background, trying to calm Tommie down. He didn't blame her. He'd been an idiot.

"Tommie, I don't want you to give away any secrets, but do you think I can convince her to forgive me and love me?" he asked slowly, realizing how much he was asking.

"Jim, she already loves you. That's why she left you."

Jim stared at the telephone receiver. Then he put it back to his ear. "She does? Are you sure?"

"Did you never talk about anything?" Tommie asked.

"No, I—I was afraid," he confessed.

Then Pete got the phone away from his wife. "You okay, Jim?" he asked.

"No. Tommie said she thinks Teresa loves me."

"Yeah, I know."

"Why didn't you tell me?"

"I figured you knew."

"No, I didn't. Pete, I've got to find her!"

"We'll find her. Together, we'll find her."

But they didn't.

For several weeks, the entire family looked for her. They had no luck.

Finally, Ann said, "Have you thought about her doctor's appointment? I'm sure she won't miss that appointment, or change doctors."

"I don't know when her next one is," Jim confessed.

"I'll call the doctor," Tommie volunteered. "I, uh,

I need an appointment and I can ask to have it at the same time as Teresa's."

Pete looked at his wife. They were all sitting in their den, talking about Teresa's disappearance.

Tommie's cheeks flushed. "I intended to tell you when we were alone, but…I think I'm pregnant."

It took Pete a moment to take in her words. Then he crossed the room in a second and held his wife against him.

Jim looked at them, wishing desperately he could hold Teresa in his arms like that.

Tommie called the doctor's office to make her appointment. When she requested to come at the same time as her sister, it took the nurse a moment to find Teresa's appointment. "She's coming in on Tuesday at three fifteen. I'll schedule you for three. How's that?"

"That would be great. Thank you very much."

When she hung up, Jim turned to Ann. "Thank you for suggesting that, Ann. I promise I'll explain everything to Teresa."

"Good. I want my girls to be happy."

Teresa felt old and tired on Tuesday. She didn't sleep well anymore, and each day was difficult. She'd thought about canceling her doctor's appointment, but she forced herself to come in. There were only a couple of women in the waiting room when she arrived, which meant the doctor wasn't too far behind. She sat down and picked up a magazine.

When the door opened again, she didn't even look up. But the new patient and her husband took the two seats next to hers, so she shifted slightly and looked up to give them a polite smile.

Then she screamed, "Tommie!" Her arms went around her sister's neck in a tight hug. "Oh, I've missed you so," she whispered.

When she sat back, she didn't even realize she was crying until Tommie took a tissue and wiped her cheeks.

"It's your fault if you missed us, silly girl," Tommie said, hugging her again. "Are you all right?"

"Yes, I'm fine."

"You look like you've lost a little weight, Teresa," Pete said.

"I'm sure I haven't. If I have, the doctor will read me the riot act."

"Well, granted, you look better than Jim," Tommie said softly.

Teresa's gaze shifted to her sister. "What about Jim?"

"He's not eating or sleeping. He's worrying about you," Pete said gently.

Tears sprang into Teresa's eyes again. "He—he needs to get used to me being gone. Then he'll be all right."

"I'm not sure about that, Teresa," Tommie said.

The nurse stepped out into the waiting room to call in the next patients. Both the other ladies went into the back with the nurse, leaving just the three of them.

Teresa suddenly focused on Tommie. "Wait! What are you doing here?"

"I think I'm pregnant," Tommie told her excitedly.

"Oh, that's wonderful! Congratulations! Our babies can play together."

"Yes, won't it be fun?"

"And thanks to you, I won't be surprised when my feet swell," Tommie said. "Though you did look cute in your wedding dress."

"Yeah, the pictures are great, Teresa," Pete agreed.

"The pictures? Of the wedding? Were they good?" Teresa asked, longing in her voice.

"Yes, they are," a deep voice said behind her.

Teresa recognized the voice, but she couldn't help turning around. She'd hungered for the sight of him ever since she'd left.

"Jim?" she said faintly.

"Yeah, it's me. Have I changed so much that you don't recognize me?"

"No, of course not!" she exclaimed, but she immediately noticed changes. Dark shadows under his eyes, a thinner face and lost weight. "You haven't been eating properly," she scolded him.

"I didn't want to eat without you there."

"You didn't want to even be there when I was," she pointed out stiffly.

Jim shot a frustrated look around the room. "We need to talk."

"That would be a change."

"Teresa—" Tommie began, but Jim shook his head. "She's right."

His blunt remark surprised both sisters.

Teresa's eyes widened. "You want a divorce?"

"Lord have mercy, no, I don't want a divorce! I'm trying to find a way to tell you I love you!" Jim said with a growl, not at all lover-like.

Teresa blinked several times. "You…love me?"

"Yeah, honey. I thought I should wait, give you time to settle in before I said anything. But it got so hard to be around you and say nothing, I started staying at the office longer so I didn't have to be with you without touching you."

Teresa reached out to his face, a soft, tender touch.

His hand covered hers and held it there against his skin.

"Teresa," he whispered, and she leaned closer to him.

"Mrs. Schofield," the nurse called from the open door.

Both Teresa and Tommie looked up.

"I think it's me," Tommie said. She and Pete stood to go into the examining room. "We'll wait for you, Teresa, after your appointment. I don't want to lose touch with you again."

Teresa smiled but said nothing.

After they left, Teresa and Jim were alone.

Jim tried again. "Teresa, will you come back and give me a chance to be the husband I should've been from the beginning?"

"But, Jim, I don't understand. Why didn't you tell me you loved me before now? You knew I loved you. I told you the night—" Her hand went to her protruding stomach.

"Because I was a coward about telling you how

much I need you. I was afraid it would make me weak if I let you know that I loved you."

"Oh, Jim." Teresa sighed, wrapping her arms around his neck and offering her lips to him.

He didn't hesitate to accept her gift. With his arms around her, he kissed her passionately, until she stopped him to remind him he was in a doctor's waiting room.

"Let's go home," Jim urged.

"I can't miss my appointment!" Teresa protested.

"Will you promise to come home with me after we see the doctor?"

"Are you sure that's what you want?"

With a grin, he said, "Didn't I convince you? I'll be glad to show you again how much I want you back."

"No, that's all right," Teresa said with a chuckle. "You convinced me. It's just that I've been miserable for so long, it's hard to believe that everything has come right."

"I hope you'll forgive me for making you miserable," Jim said, his voice serious.

"It's not all your fault, Jim. I have to bear some responsibility for seducing you." Her cheeks flushed.

"As I remember that evening, honey, you didn't have to work too hard to convince me. It's a delightful memory I'll always treasure. And the result is our boys, so there's a happy ending, right?"

With his arm around her, his warmth, his scent surrounding her, all Teresa could say was, "Oh, yes."

Jim kissed her forehead. "It may have taken us awhile to straighten everything out, but we're finally a family."

"Mr. and Mrs. Schofield," the nurse called, summoning them to an examination room.

Jim stood and helped Teresa up. "Come on, honey, let's go talk to the doctor so we can go home."

That was exactly what she wanted.

Epilogue

"Jim?" Teresa said softly when he picked up his phone. "It's time!"

"Time for what, honey?" he said, his mind on his work.

"I need to go to the hospital."

That got his attention. "But it's not time yet."

Teresa laughed. "Yes, it is. The doctor said to get there at once. My water broke."

"I'll be right there!"

Half an hour later, Teresa was in the labor room with Jim holding her hand.

"Does it hurt too much?" he asked, leaning over her.

"No, it's not too— Aigh!" she screamed.

"That came faster this time, didn't it?"

A nurse came in and moved him out of the way.

"Step outside. I'll let you know when you can come back in."

Jim moved to the waiting room, surprised to find it filled with their families. "I forgot to call. How did you know?"

"Teresa got me at the office while she was waiting for you," Tommie said. "I called everyone else."

"How is she?" Ann asked. "Has the doctor said anything about the babies coming early?"

"He told her last week that any time now they'd be safe," Jim said. He looked at Tommie. "Did you get your sonogram done?"

"Yes, we're just having one and it's a girl," Tommie said happily.

The nurse came out to summon him. "Sir, you can come back in. We're going to delivery right away. You'll need to get into scrubs now."

Jim hurried. He'd promised Teresa he'd be there for the delivery. They were in this together. The last few months had been wonderful. He wasn't sure why he'd feared marriage so much, but with Teresa, everything was wonderful.

In his scrubs, he reached Teresa's side.

"I thought you'd decided not to come," she said through open-mouthed pants.

"No, sweetheart. I'm here. How are we doing?"

"It's time!"

"All right, Teresa," the doctor said. "It's time to push."

With encouragement from Jim and Dr. Benson, Teresa gave birth to their long-awaited sons. The nurses cleaned up the babies, wrapped them in blankets and put pale-blue knitted caps on their little heads.

Teresa held one in each arm. "Aren't they wonderful?" she asked in awe.

"No more wonderful than their courageous mother. I'm a very lucky man."

"We're both lucky, Jim, because we found each other. I can't imagine another man I'd want to share my life with."

"Me, too, sweetheart," he said, bending to kiss her. "Now, what are we naming them?"

"Number one is Thomas Michael. Number two is Jonathan James. I hope we can keep them straight."

"We'll manage."

And they did.

* * * * *

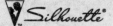

This September,

SPECIAL EDITION™

brings you the third book in
the exciting new continuity

Eleven students.
One reunion.
And a secret that will
change everyone's lives.

THE MEASURE OF A MAN
(SE #1706)

by award-winning author

MARIE FERRARELLA

Jane Johnson had worked at her alma mater for several
years before the investigation into her boss, Professor
Gilbert Harrison, put her job at risk. Desperate to keep her
income, Jane begged her former classmate Smith Parker
to help her find secret information that could exonerate
the professor. Smith was reluctant—he wanted to stay
out of trouble—but he couldn't resist the charms of the
beautiful single mom. The hours they spent together soon
led to intense sparks...and all-out passion. But when an
old secret threatens Smith's job—and his reputation—will
the fallout put an end to their happiness forever?

*Don't miss this compelling story—
only from Silhouette Books.*

Available at your favorite retail outlet.

If you enjoyed what you just read,
then we've got an offer you can't resist!

Take 2 bestselling
love stories FREE!
Plus get a FREE surprise gift!

HARLEQUIN®

Coming this September

In the first of Charlotte Douglas's Maggie Skerritt mysteries, an experienced police detective has to predict a serial killer's next move while charting her course for the future. But will Maggie's longtime friend and confidant add another life-altering event to the mix?

PELICAN BAY
Charlotte Douglas

SILHOUETTE *Romance*

COMING NEXT MONTH

#1786 MUCH ADO ABOUT MATCHMAKING—
Myrna Mackenzie
Shakespeare in Love
Can the stage for love really be set by a well-intentioned
matchmaker's trickery, a villainous relative and a gorgeous hotel?
Independent, career-minded Emmaline Carstairs wants little to do
with ex-military businessman Ryan Benedict. Still, the roles her
uncle coerces them into playing seem more natural every moment…
and a wedding might just be the final act!

#1787 THE TEXAN'S SUITE ROMANCE—
Judy Christenberry
Lone Star Brides
Filling in as a publicist, Tabitha Tyler finds herself butting heads
with writer Alex Myerson as they embark on a book tour. But as
traveling difficulties bring them closer, Tabitha begins to see another
side to Alex. And it's not long before she embarks on her most
difficult campaign to date—convincing the widowed author
to start a new chapter in his life with her.

#1788 LIGHTS, ACTION…FAMILY!—Patricia Thayer
Love at the Goodtime Café
Hired to be a stuntman for a movie being shot on her family ranch,
Reece McKellen instantly attracts Emily Hunter's eye. And it's
not long before their off-screen chemistry has Emily wondering if
the handsome stranger and his niece might not provide the most
important scene in her life.…

#1789 HER GYPSY PRINCE—Crystal Green
Blossom County Fair
The Gypsy Prince captivated Elizabeth Dupres immediately, even as
she picketed his carnival. Although they came from vastly different
worlds, she is powerless to deny her attraction to him. And now
Elizabeth must decide if she will let this wandering man walk out of
her life forever or stand up to her family to embrace his love.

SRCNM0905